Out of the Depths

Also by Leonard Holton

FLOWERS BY REQUEST

DELIVER US FROM WOLVES

SECRET OF THE DOUBTING SAINT

A PACT WITH SATAN

THE SAINT MAKER

Out of the Depths

LEONARD HOLTON

Dodd, Mead & Company
NEW YORK

Printed in the United States of America
by The Haddon Craftsmen, Inc., Scranton, Penna.

One

IT WAS MIDSUMMER and Father Joseph Bredder, O.F.M., delighting both in the warmth of the Southern California sun and the cool touch of the northwest breeze, was leaning on the railing of the Hermosa Beach Pier vaguely hoping to catch a halibut. It was Wednesday and his day of leisure, and instead of spending it in the garden of the Convent of the Holy Innocents in downtown Los Angeles, he had come to Hermosa Beach to fish. His friend, Lieutenant Minardi of the Los Angeles Police Department, was fishing beside him and was a better fisherman, for he had caught two fish already—a small halibut and a large bonita.

"Fishing calls for the exercise of at least two of the cardinal virtues," said Minardi, in good spirits because of his catch. "Prudence and fortitude." He glanced at a fat man to his left, surreptitiously taking a drink of whisky from a small bottle concealed in a paper bag. "To that you might add temperance," he concluded. "Hello, Shiny," he said to the fat man. "What brings you here?"

The fat man turned his blotched red face on the detective and said, "I don't have to answer that, gumshoe."

Minardi shook his head sadly. "You haven't the talent

to be a lawbreaker, Shiny," he said. "Too aggressive, too hostile. Those with a minimum of hostility are most likely to succeed. Put that bottle away. You are setting a bad example to juveniles and violating a city ordinance."

For answer, Shiny flung the bottle, which was empty now, into the ocean and the paper bag with it, and shuffled off down the pier. The crushed paper bag floated sadly on the glittering water.

"He worries me," said Minardi, giving a little tug at his line to liven up his bait.

"Why?" asked Father Bredder.

"Wrong place," said Minardi. "Shiny is strictly a downtown character—Main Street and East Los Angeles, that's his natural habitat. Rolling drunks, illegal bookmaking, the cruder forms of confidence tricks—those are his activities. He doesn't go with pier fishing and these surroundings."

"It's a mistake to type people," said Father Bredder. "Between the individual and the type into which he is put there is a world of difference. You've forgotten Gilbert and Sullivan.

> *"When the enterprising burglar's not a-burgling*
> *And the cut-throat isn't occupied in crime*
> *He loves to hear the little brook a-gurgling*
> *And listen to the merry village chime."*

"Maybe," said Minardi, and eyed his companion thoughtfully. Father Bredder was clad in blue jeans and a blue workshirt, both old but well laundered and neatly patched. He was a man built on a large plan, well over six feet, with broad shoulders and thick and muscular

2 ·

arms. He would be mistaken for a truck driver or a construction worker, but he was actually chaplain of the Holy Innocents Convent. Before that he had been a sergeant in the United States Marine Corps. He had a professional knowledge of hand-to-hand combat, was an excellent boxer and wrestler and, before entering the Marines in World War II, had played semipro ball at some remote hamlet called Twin Oaks, Ohio. He was also a very humble man and acutely shy, and all this was belied by his truck driver exterior.

Between the type which Father Bredder represented and the individual man there was then, indeed, a world of difference.

"I've got a bite," he said.

"Don't jerk," pleaded Minardi, full of the anxieties of the devoted fisherman. "Let him take the hook. Give him some slack." Since the priest was slow to react, Minardi reached over, took Father Bredder's line and pulled several feet of it off the reel against the brake. Then he gave the taunt line a gentle tug and felt something heavy and sluggish on the end.

"Halibut," he said. "They like to mouth the bait and then spit it out and take it in again. Give him a few minutes to swallow it. Then reel in. Firmly and slowly. You don't have to strike. He'll take the hook right down inside."

The priest followed these instructions, his hand on the reel so big that the reel seemed to be but a toy. The fishing pole arched and the tip bent in a graceful dip under the strain.

Minardi eyed it keenly and was disappointed. "Kelp,"

he said. "Keep winding." The line suddenly gave and came in more readily.

"I lost it," said Father Bredder. "But there's still some there."

"Weed," said the detective. "There's still some on the hook. Bring it on in and we'll get you a fresh bait."

It wasn't kelp that was on the end of Father Bredder's line, but a black shiny shape made of rubber and in the form of a sock. Even before it broke the surface of the water, the smell from it was abominable and those around the priest started to back away. Minardi stared at the object for a moment. There was a whitish glistening substance inside the curious rubber sock.

"Let it go," he said so fiercely that the priest was startled. "Let it back into the water." He took the rod from his friend and released the brake on the reel so that the odious rubber thing went to the bottom.

"What was it?" asked the priest.

Minardi didn't reply. He had, because of his profession, noted a local policeman on duty by a kiosk which sold bait and tackle and he went over to him, said a few swift words, and the policeman started to clear the end of the pier of fishermen and idlers. Minardi entered a phone booth by the kiosk, dialed a number, spoke for less than a minute and then returned to the priest who was standing, bewildered, by his rod and line.

"What's this all about?" asked Father Bredder.

"I think it's about a body down there," said Minardi. "What you had on your line was a neoprene rubber bootie belonging to a scuba diver. And it looked as if the diver's foot was inside."

Father Bredder had expected that a police car with a moaning siren would soon drive up the pier toward them, through the press of people who were now herded together halfway down the structure. But instead a fast powerboat approached from the sea and, dashing in toward the head of the pier, pivoted around and let go an anchor. Besides the helmsman there were two others on board, already dressed in the black rubber suits of scuba divers. When the boat came to anchor, they laboriously put air tanks on their backs, fastened on weight belts, and the helmsman hailed the priest.

"You the man that found the sinker?" he asked.

"Yes," said Father Bredder, guessing at what was meant by sinker.

"Whereabouts was your line in the water when you started reeling in?"

"About right under you," said the priest.

"Okay," said the helmsman. He turned to the two divers and with a downward gesture of his thumb signaled them to get into the water. They seemed in no hurry. They spat in their faceplates, dipped them over the side and washed them out in sea water, and put them in position. They pulled on rubber mittens, put their mouthpieces in place, and took a few tentative sucks.

One of them picked up a roll of half-inch line and attached one end of it to a cleat on the launch. Then they peered at each other for a few seconds like a couple of beings from another planet, nodded the one to the other, sat on the side of the launch with their backs to the water and tumbled backward into the ocean, like a couple of humpty-dumpties falling together off a wall.

They hit the water with a tremendous splash on the near side of the launch and a cloud of lively greenish bubbles marked the spot where they had disappeared.

The priest found the whole performance exciting. He was not much of a swimmer himself, and his only underwater experience had been diving from a small clay cliff into an abandoned excavation on a farm which provided a swimming hole during his boyhood in Ohio. He had always kept his eyes shut when diving, but once opened them and saw on the bottom a murky green world with dark smeared objects which were boulders. The sight had both frightened and fascinated him, but he had never had the nerve to open his eyes underwater again. Yet here were two people exploring the bottom of the sea, looking for a drowned man who had been wearing the same equipment which they carried and which had presumably failed him. He found that he was holding his breath, waiting for the divers to reappear.

"Relax," said Minardi. "They're professionals—part of the Body Recovery Unit of the County Lifeguards."

"Why did they take the line down with them?" asked the priest.

"To help search," said Minardi. "It's gloomy down there. Probably no more than ten feet visibility or so. They hold the line and swim along the bottom making a circle around the launch. That way they don't lose their bearings and can be sure they are not covering the same area."

"Have you ever done this?" asked the priest.

"I started to learn," said the detective. "But I chickened out. I figured that there are enough hazards in my business without taking on any that are unneeded."

"It's really dangerous?"

"You have to know what you're doing. If you know what you're doing at all times, they say it isn't dangerous. But people panic or get careless. They get tangled in kelp or run out of air and do the wrong thing, and that's usually the end for them. Some are never found. This one probably got tangled and panicked and has turned up to provide an end to our day's fishing."

It was about three in the afternoon and the sun was still high in the sky though headed west toward Point Dume further up the coast, where it would set. Under the bright sunlight the ocean's surface had a lively, dancing look and Father Bredder was struck by the contrast of the loveliness of the sea and the horror which lay beneath it only a few yards from where he stood on the pier. There was much in life like that—loveliness and horror side by side, good and evil, and between these two mankind, confused and half blind, but reaching toward that which was good. He saw the tip of the pole bend and then jerk and Minardi, noticing it, grimaced.

"They're cutting your catch off," he said. "Maybe they found the rest of him now." The lone policeman was doing his best to keep the crowd off the pierhead but, spurred by the excitement of seeing something gruesome, several had slipped up the far side of the pier and joined the priest and the detective by the rail. Among them was the fat, red-faced man known as Shiny.

"What's cooking?" he demanded of Minardi, apparently forgetting their previous passage. "What's going on?"

"They're looking for a body," said Minardi.

· 7

"Get back there," said the policeman, pushing at one or two of those who had drifted to the pierhead.

"What's wrong about looking?" demanded Shiny.

"It's morally bad for you to satisfy that kind of curiosity," said Minardi. "Come on, Shiny. Move back. You others, too."

"Who do you think you are?" demanded one. "A cop?"

"Right the first time," said Minardi. "You want to move, or you want to be arrested for interfering with an officer?"

The little mob moved back resentfully.

"Funny thing about crowds," said Minardi. "Speak authoritatively and they obey you—for a little while."

"I think they're coming up," said Father Bredder. The seething bubbles of the divers disturbed the surface with a cauldron flow, and first one and then the other black-clad head emerged. One of the divers took his mouth-piece out and shouted to the man on the boat.

"Give us a couple of bags—big ones." The helmsman handed two or three glittering plastic bags to the diver, who replaced his mouthpiece and disappeared with his companion. They were down this time only four or five minutes and then surfaced, carrying one of the bags between them. It contained a large black lump.

They went down and came back with three more bags, each with a horrid relic, and then they climbed on board, but first passed up a diver's tank, weight belt and regulator. The tank was heavily encrusted with barnacles and weed.

When they themselves got on board, they sat very

wearily on the side of the launch and took off their fins and face plates and tanks as if utterly spent. One of them leaned forward over the water and either retched or spat copiously. Then they got up and helped spread a tarpaulin over the bags which had been placed in the rear of the cruiser.

"That's it, Joe," said the helmsman to the policeman on the pier. He turned to Minardi and the priest. "You two guys come on down to lifeguard headquarters."

"Any idea who it was?" shouted the policeman.

The helmsman shrugged. "Some smart aleck diving alone," he said, and went forward to get the anchor in on the power winch. Then he gunned the accelerator, and the cruiser shot off in a lovely patch of white foam of its own making.

Two

"You keep forgetting that I am a specialist," said Minardi. "Death of any kind interests you, but I am only interested in death of a particular kind, that is to say, death at the hands of a fellow human being, and then only if premeditated or planned. So I never did bother to inquire, though there should have been an item in the papers about it by now."

Father Bredder looked embarrassed. Because he was a shy man, he didn't like to visit Minardi at police headquarters, and he hadn't really been intending to do so. But he had been walking past the headquarters two days after their fishing trip and on the spur of the moment he had gone in through the beautiful plate-glass doors with the aluminum trim that made the place look more like a hotel than the headquarters of a law-enforcement agency, and here he was in Minardi's office asking about the body of the drowned diver.

"I was just curious," said the priest.

"Join the human race," said Minardi with a faint smile. "Look," he continued. "I've been busy with something else and forgot all about your diver. But I'm glad you called in, because I want you to do something for me. So hold on and I'll satisfy your curiosity and then maybe you can do me a favor."

He picked up the telephone, dialed a number quickly and then said, "Hello. Hermosa Beach Police? Lieutenant Minardi of Los Angeles here. Listen. You remember that sinker they pulled up off the end of the pier? Got any identification?" He listened awhile, scribbling rapidly on a piece of paper and then said, "Thanks a lot. No. Just curious. Thanks." Then he rang off.

"No identification," he said, looking at his scribbled notes. "That is, no individual identification. Male, about thirty-six years of age, weighed about one hundred eighty pounds, no water in the lungs. Died of something called air embolism, whatever that is. Maybe what people call bends. Body been in the water from three weeks to a month. Badly chewed about by fish and crabs. That's about it."

"That's curious," said Father Bredder.

"What's curious?"

"No identification."

"Not curious at all," said Minardi. "When a body has been underwater for that length of time, about all the identification left is the teeth, and that takes a long, long time. Maybe months before they find out who he was."

"But surely not that many people disappear diving?" said Father Bredder.

Minardi gave him a patient, sad smile. "When people disappear, nobody knows what they were doing," he said. "If we knew what they were doing at the time they disappeared, then they wouldn't disappear. You'd be surprised at the number who disappear every day just in Los

Angeles. We have a whole section of the police department looking for them and we don't find more than twenty per cent. Missing persons. It's one of our biggest jobs. When I worked in Missing Persons, I used to think that maybe the world really was flat after all, and people just took a walk and fell off the edge."

"What I mean," said Father Bredder, "is that surely not that many people who dive disappear. Diving is a pretty limited field as a hobby. A diver would be known to other divers somewhere and his disappearance would be reported."

"He may not have been a real diver," said Minardi. "He may have been just somebody who watched television and saw the divers fooling around in the water with a porpoise like Flipper and decided he'd like to try it himself. So he borrowed or rented some gear and jumped in and drowned himself."

"Or got air whatever-it-was."

"That's right," said Minardi. "Or got air whatever-it-was. Which would support the theory that he wasn't a real diver in the first place."

"It's still odd," said Father Bredder. "Somebody must have missed him and reported him missing."

"Maybe they did," said Minardi patiently. "Look. Suppose he came from some inland town like Duarte. He decided to try diving and killed himself at Hermosa Beach. His friend in Duarte reports he is missing. Now just try to figure how long it would be for the man reported missing in Duarte to be identified as the body found in a diver's suit off the Hermosa Beach Pier. Every person reported missing has to be matched against every unidentified body found. It sometimes takes months. So forget it."

"He must have left his clothes somewhere," said Father Bredder.

Minardi sighed. "Okay, Father. I see it's no use. Go ahead and work on your little fishing mystery. Meanwhile, come with me and have a cup of coffee and listen to my troubles. I've got plenty."

It was typical of Minardi that whenever he wanted to talk confidentially to Father Bredder, he did so, not in the security of his own cubicle of an office, but in a rundown drugstore on Main Street, which was a remnant of the old drab center of Los Angeles now largely replaced by glittering federal, county, state, and city buildings. This drugstore was the only ready source of coffee and snacks in the neighborhood, for those who had planned the new city center, with its block buildings of steel and glass, had forgotten that the tens of thousands of employees working there would need coffee and doughnuts at odd times in order to carry on their work of jailing people, taxing people, marrying people, paying them old-age pensions or selling them postage.

The rundown drugstore was owned by a Mexican with the un-Mexican name of Marty. He was a huge mound of pale fat who shuffled about painfully behind a long gloomy counter serving his customers slowly and with deliberation. He moved as if movement caused him pain, and Father Bredder had often thought that he must have been born with broken-down feet. Even to watch Marty shuffle about made the priest wince.

In this unlikely spot all who had official business came

at some time during the day for coffee—attorneys and tax collectors, judges and plaintiffs, sheriffs, police officers and breathless couples who had just been issued their marriage licenses. The coffee was vile and the doughnuts, even in the morning, looked as if someone had been licking the sugar off them. The hamburgers were served on buns so soft as to be nauseating, and a patina of grease seemed to cover everything in the establishment. Yet Marty's was the only haven from the gigantic official machinery around, and it was to Marty's that Lieutenant Minardi took Father Bredder, and having said "Hi" to a superior court judge who was reading a *Racing Form* in the corner, and another "Hi" to an official of the Alien Tax Division, Department of Internal Revenue, who was wiping the crumbs of stale doughnut off his well-pressed dark suit, he steered Father Bredder to a booth at the end of the counter and held up two fingers for coffee.

"Ever hear of Intersystems Technology Incorporated?" he asked.

"No," said Father Bredder, reaching for his pipe. He got it with the difficulty that a big man always experiences in trying to get into his trousers pockets while sitting down. It was an old black brier, and with it Father Bredder produced a crumpled envelope which he opened very carefully. He filled his pipe from it with dark Carolina tobacco.

"For goodness' sakes," said Minardi, "haven't you got a tobacco pouch yet?"

"I got one last Christmas," said Father Bredder.

"From Cagey Charlie. But I lost it." Cagey Charlie was a broken-down boxer and a friend of the priest's.

"Look," said Minardi, "I know about vows of poverty and all that. But don't they give you enough money to buy a tobacco pouch?"

"Oh, yes," said the priest. "We're not paupers. I think it would be better if we could be. But something happened to the world, and there are bus fares to pay, and so on. So we get an ample allowance. Much more than we need, really."

"How much?" asked Minardi.

"Thirty dollars a month."

"Tax-free, I suppose," said Minardi dryly. "You can get a tobacco pouch right here at Marty's for twenty-five cents."

"That isn't the point," said Father Bredder. "You see, the thirty dollars is to be spent on necessities. Sometimes I have to take a bus or make a telephone call. That's what it is for. Anything left over I can spend on my personal pleasures."

"I give," said Minardi. "Let's get back to Intersystems Technology. They are part of the gung-ho space boom— the boys from Caltech and Massachusetts Institute of Technology who sell figures to the people who contract to make the rockets we keep flinging up into the air. They can calculate things like the potential path of a raindrop from five thousand feet to the leaf it well hit on a tree when coming down over Exposition Park with the wind blowing at fifteen miles an hour from the northwest. This kind of information begins to get mountainous after a while, and stuff that is practical gets lost among stuff that has no immediate use. Intersystems keeps its fingers on all the calculation techniques, as it were, and digs out the useful ones. It's an old company. Five years old, in fact. That's close to ancient in this space stuff."

"And the president of the company has been shot?" asked Father Bredder, lighting his pipe.

"Father, don't be corny," said Minardi. "Not the president—the janitor. And he wasn't shot. He died of a perfectly normal heart attack—if a heart attack can be described as normal. That's the medical report, and the autopsy was done by Simms, who is a first-rate pathologist. Angina pectoris is the old name for it—a clot of blood breaks loose from the walls of the arteries or somewhere and blocks the heart, and that's it. If help arrives immediately, the patient can often be saved. But Bodetkin—Paul Bodetkin—that's the janitor—had his attack driving to work on the Pacific Coast Highway, and by the time they got him to the hospital, it was too late."

"I'm sorry he died," said the priest simply. "But why are you interested in the case?"

"Idiot mail," said Minardi. "We got three separate letters in the usual block capitals saying that he was actually murdered. We get idiot mail all the time and have to check it out. Normally it's just routine. But since Bodetkin worked for Intersystems, we have to pay special attention and it has been handed to me."

"What can I do?" asked Father Bredder.

"Without making a fuss, find out all you can about Bodetkin: who were his friends, where he ate, whether he had a girl friend, what were his hobbies, how much money he spent, and where. All that sort of stuff. He lived in your parish, and with your contacts it shouldn't be difficult. Only don't make a fuss. That's important."

Father Bredder actually didn't have a parish. He was chaplain to the Convent of the Holy Innocents in downtown Los Angeles a little distance from Main Street. But before this appointment, he had been attached to St. Vibiana's Cathedral, and there his parish had been the scruffy Main Street and east side of Los Angeles, and he had a wide acquaintance among the winoes, tipsters, and hangers-on who made up the broken but fascinating population of Los Angeles' Skid Row. These still regarded him as their own and brought him whatever problems they thought he could solve. When he wanted information, they got it for him.

"All right," said Father Bredder. "But I don't understand all this fuss about a janitor."

"He's a space age janitor," said Minardi with a touch of sarcasm. "He had to have about as much clearance as a secret serviceman to get the job. That's what's special about him."

"You think Bodetkin was murdered in spite of the autopsy?" asked Father Bredder.

"No, I don't," said Minardi. "But I have to show, putting the medical report aside, that his death was not, let us say, convenient. That he left the world clean and honest and with nothing hidden—particularly anything that would involve Intersystems Technology. That is this space stuff for you." He signaled to Marty to replenish their cups, and fished a packet of cigarettes out of his pocket. They were filter tips and he broke off the filter and lit one of the cigarettes.

"Why do you buy filter tips and then break off the filters?" asked Father Bredder.

"I like strong cigarettes with plenty of nicotine and tars," said Minardi. "You know that stuff about the flavor getting throught the filters? Well, the only way that can be done in my book is if the tobacco is stronger. With this brand, break off the filter and you've got a cigarette that would choke a crow. And that's how I like them."

Marty shuffled over with the coffeepot and leaned heavily on the table while he filled their cups.

"Your coffee gets worse every day, Marty," said Minardi.

"With the kind of custom we get in here it don't make any difference," said Marty, "They got so much on their minds they can't even taste it." He lowered his voice. "You got something big on, Lieutenant?" he asked.

"No. Why?"

"That guy behind you is real interested in what you been saying."

Minardi slowly turned around and looked straight at the man. He was a big man, dressed in a dark suit, and pretending, at the moment, to be reading a paper.

"You got a match?" he asked.

The man was more surprised than he should have been by the request. "Match?" he repeated. "Yes. I think I have." He fumbled in his pocket and produced a book of matches.

"Thanks," said Minardi, lit a cigarette and, ignoring the other's outstretched hand, put the matches in his pocket. They finished their coffee and went out.

"Whoever he was, if he was listening, he isn't much good at it," said the dectective.

"Why do you say that?" asked the priest.

"He gave me his fingerprints when he gave me the matches," said Minardi. "Strictly an amateur."

Three

SINCE THIS WAS the summer vacation, there was not a
great deal of work for Father Bredder to do in connection with the Convent of the Holy Innocents. He had no
classes to hold and no problems to solve or at least listen
to in connection with the girls of the convent. He missed
the students, because when he was tired or downcast over
his own insufficiencies, they revived him by their presence. There was a freshness and a joy about the children
at the convent, an honesty and vivacity that revived him
without fail, and since he had been chaplain at the convent, he had come to understand on a deeper level that
admonition of his Master that to enter the kingdom of
Heaven, one must become a child again.

"Adults," he said to Father Armstrong, his assistant,
"forget about joy. Even in their approach to God they
tend to be guilty and miserable. Children are much more
wholesome. To them God is as real and happy a concept
as baseball, and that's right, because baseball is part of
God and . . ." He stopped there because whenever he
tried to put into words his feelings about God, the words
seemed inadequate. The concept was too great, too
overwhelming, for words.

"If this is some kind of a play to get me to take a more active part in the girls' softball and basketball program during the coming year, I reject it," said Father Armstrong. "I dislike athletics, and my concept of Purgatory is some kind of a place where people have to play organized games all the time.

"By the way, while you were out, you had a telephone call from a Dr. Tighler. The number's on a piece of paper on your desk there. He wanted you to call as soon as you returned."

"Dr. Tighler?" said Father Bredder. "I don't know anyone by that name."

Father Armstrong shrugged. "He was insistent that you call him immediately," he said. The prefix of the telephone number was Crestview, indicating a fashionable address in West Los Angeles or Beverly Hills. Father Bredder dialed the number, asked for Dr. Tighler, giving his own name, and was kept waiting for a while before Dr. Tighler came to the telephone.

"Forgive my intruding on you," said Dr. Tighler. "I need to see you—as soon as possible. It is very important."

"Where are you?" asked Father Bredder.

"North Canyon Drive, Beverly Hills. About a half hour's drive from downtown Los Angeles."

"Wouldn't a priest closer by be able to help you?"

"Priest?" said Dr. Tighler. "I don't want to talk to a priest. I want to talk to you—confidentially."

"But I am a priest," said Father Bredder.

"Quite so. But I want to talk to you in your other capacity—that of a private investigator. I cannot tell you

· *21*

anything beyond that I am connected with work of national importance—grave national importance—and I have a problem which cannot be handled through regular governmental or police channels."

"I am sorry, Dr. Tighler," said Father Bredder. "But I am not available as a private investigator and I cannot do anything for you. Whatever your problem, I am sure that there are others to whom you should turn."

There was now an awkward silence. Dr. Tighler, rejected, was trying to recover his balance, and Father Bredder, having done the rejecting, was hoping that he had not appeared rude or pompous.

"I don't seem to be making my point," said Dr. Tighler, ending the strained silence. "I am quite aware that there are many official agencies available to me. I can tell you nothing further on the telephone except that I need your services and nobody else's, and the matter in which I need them is critical to the national defense. I am not given to hysterics and I would not be calling you unless it was absolutely necessary."

"Are you a doctor of medicine?" asked Father Bredder.

"Heavens no. I am a physicist."

"Let me call you back, Dr. Tighler," said Father Bredder. "I cannot see you until this evening, in any case. As you know, I am a priest and I do not like to enter any kind of detective work."

"But you have done investigatory work in the past," said Dr. Tighler.

"Only when there has been some spiritual need involved," said Father Bredder. "Would that be so in your case?"

"Spiritual need?" echoed Dr. Tighler. "Spiritual need?" There was an edge of irritation in his voice. "I don't think you are the man I require," he said. "I've been misinformed. I will get someone else. Forgive my troubling you," and he rang off.

Father Bredder gave a rueful smile and turned to Father Armstrong, who, being in the same room, had caught half the conversation.

"Why do they shy away from the work 'spiritual'?" he asked.

"Bigotry, my dear fellow," replied Father Armstrong cheerfully. "Pure bigotry parading as learning . . . as it always does. We have entered the spiritual Dark Ages. Or perhaps we never really got out of them. Six hundred years ago people used to recite little rhymes to ward off the Devil, and now they recite little equations, and with the same objective. What is called Science has replaced God and Devil, and men's souls are reckoned nonexistent because they cannot be found with photoelectrical equipment."

Father Armstrong was an Englishman who had attended seminaries in Belgium, Spain and Ireland and then, having received Holy Orders, had taken his doctorate in English letters at Oxford. He was a slim, fair-haired, young-looking man with a dry wit, the manners of a diplomat, and a depth of learning far beyond that of the older priest. He was sure of himself in all circumstances, and Father Bredder admired this quality, feeling inadequate and unfit in many situations. He looked disturbed, both perplexed and hurt, and Father Armstrong was surprised at this reaction.

"Come, Father," he said, to atone for his somewhat flip answer, "you surely realize that what is going on in the world today is a struggle between the spirit of man and the mind of man. The two are reckoned to be irreconcilable, and so those who follow the path of the mind reject the spirit in self-defense. They look only for what can be proved, and since all things provable must be finite, must be containable in a definition, our field of eternity and immortality is, for them, anathema." He paused. "I gather your Dr. Tighler was looking for a detective."

"Yes, he was," said Father Bredder. "He certainly wasn't looking for a priest."

"Ah," said Father Armstrong. "In that case, what he probably needs is a priest. Often what we are looking for is quite different from what we need. It is a paradox, and that is the way it works. Are you going to see him?"

"No. He decided, when I mentioned the word spiritual, that he didn't want me."

"Which of course means that actually he does," said Father Armstrong. "Well, you have his number, so you will be able to get in touch with him."

But Father Bredder, now shaken over the rectitude of his answer to Dr. Tighler's request, decided to think the matter over more deeply. Meanwhile, he set out to find what he could about the janitor, Paul Bodetkin, for his friend, Lieutenant Minardi.

Bodetkin had lived at the Porter Hotel on Broadway near Sixth Street, not far from the Convent of the Holy

Innocents. The priest knew the hotel well. At one time, situated in the center of Los Angeles, it had been an eminently respectable residential hotel—not lavish or splendid, but solid and comfortable, with a sensible menu, quiet rooms, a decent lounge and no cocktail bar. It had struggled since its opening to maintain its position, but had gradually declined as a result of the deterioration of the center of the city around it.

Business and professional people of means no longer kept rooms at the Porter. Its clients were now elderly people in reduced circumstances and salesmen for modest companies who were not required to put up a good front to sell their goods or services.

The hotel was still eminently decent, but it was poor and out at the elbows. The carpet in the lounge was close to threadbare. In the coffee room there were gray, napless areas down the center and near the little service elevator, and these worn spots the management could not afford to repair.

And yet the hotel was quiet and neat. The doorman had been on the staff thirty years, and many of the waiters a decade or more. The manager, Mr. Ambrose, a man in his late fifties, had occupied that position for fifteen years, but had been on the staff of the hotel, coming up through the kitchen, since he was eighteen.

Father Bredder saw him in a dark office which lay behind the modest hotel desk. Possibly when the hotel had been built, the office had been designed to convey an impression of subdued light and the serenity and dignity which went with its condition. But the years had reduced this atmosphere to one of dullness and chill. The mahogany desk, once a handsome piece, was now scuffed about the sides, and the tan carpet was blotched through the decomposition of the dyes. The heavy drapes on the windows had something of the character of shrouds.

The only item of dignity in the office was Mr. Ambrose himself—silver-haired, with a complexion as pink as the tiny rose he wore in his buttonhole, well-kept hands and scrupulously polished shoes. He was not dapper. He was, instead, correct, crisp, clean and still human. The priest saw in Mr. Ambrose, the manager, the soul, as it were, of the hotel, still bright, still self-respecting, despite the deterioration of the body.

"It's nice to see you, Father," said Mr. Ambrose, for the two knew each other, the connecting link being the hotelier's daughter Cynthia, aged twelve, who was a student at the Convent. "Try the leather chair—it's the most comfortable—and I will call for some lemonade—unless you prefer tea?"

"Lemonade will be fine," said the priest. "It is a little hot outside."

"Not the humidity but the glare," said Mr. Ambrose. "That is what kills our city—a desert glare on concrete, glass and tarmac is extremely trying on the nerves. It occurs to me that many of the eccentricities attributed to the people of Los Angeles may be traceable to the nervous irritation brought about by the glare around the city —a striking, blinding, visual affliction that seems to be increasing. Of course, we get less breeze in the city now because of the extent of our high buildings. When I first came here, thirty-two years ago, we got quite a nice ocean breeze in the afternoon. But no longer. We are all, as it were, half baked," and he gave a little chuckle at his own witticism.

Father Bredder had no small talk himself, none of the social subtleties and, faced with the task of getting some information concerning a former guest of the hotel, could find no way of doing this other than by a direct approach.

The lemonade arrived. Mr. Ambrose took a grateful sip of his, put the glass delicately on the desk and said, "Cynthia is away with her aunt in Laguna Beach. I miss her. But she will be back in a week or two. She has troubles with her Latin, as you perhaps know, and wants to give it up in favor of Spanish. But I am not happy with the thought. The decline in the study of the classics can have a serious effect on our civilization. It is from the Greeks and the Romans and the Jews that we derive our principles—our sense of justice, our sense of ethics. Throw the classical studies out and we lose our roots. We will change, and for the worse. We will cease to be guided by principles and will make all our decisions on particular cases, and so be lost. One sees this happening even now in our courts and our legislatures, where decisions are made to provide for a particular group without regard to the benefit of society as a whole. No. Cynthia must stick to her Latin. She prefers Spanish for the wrong reason—because it is easier."

"Latin is a good discipline," said Father Bredder, glad to be able to make some contribution. "Father Armstrong says that nothing is worth learning that is not hard to learn. He teaches Latin," he added. Father Bredder was not very good at Latin himself. He could read Latin and translate into Latin, but had not the facility and elegance in the language of Father Armstrong, who maintained that the key to all languages lay in the discipline of Latin grammar.

"Well, Latin it will be for Cynthia," said Mr. Ambrose. "Ovid at the next semester, I think. I like him. He was a sort of Roman Robert Frost. But you perhaps have some little problem of your own, and I waste your time with chatter about my daughter. Is there anything I can do to help you?"

"I think you had a man staying here by the name of Paul Bodetkin," said Father Bredder.

"Bodetkin? Of course. Room three-twelve. It's really a small suite—bedroom with a little sitting room and kitchenette. A nice man, but not the very best kind of hotel guest—though one should speak well of the dead. You know he is dead, of course?"

"Yes," said Father Bredder. "Why do you say he was not the best kind of hotel guest?"

"Untidy I think is the word," said Mr. Ambrose. "Untidy in his thinking and in his living. For instance, we have hours for breakfast, lunch and dinner, but he seemed incapable of remembering them—always late or early for mealtimes, so that he ate a great deal in his room and wasn't very scrupulous about tidying up. Of course, our chambermaids straighten up the rooms each day and clean them also. Yet one needs a little co-operation from guests, and Bodetkin was not above leaving cans of sardines on his coffee table or strewing crumbs all over his carpet.

"Then he had hobbies that caused a nuisance. Photography was one. He did his own developing and printing and got the chemicals on the carpet and furniture, so I had to talk several times to him about it. He used some kind of high-powered floodlamps that once or twice blew fuses on his floor. Psychologically, he was quite a puzzle. He was a very inoffensive man, never brusque or angry with the help. And yet he lived without consideration for others. He never thought of the chambermaids who had to clean up his room. He never thought of the guest adjacent who didn't want to hear Prokofiev's 'Second' at eleven o'clock at night.

"He never thought of the kitchen staff who could not provide him with a meal after hours. And so on. Not deliberate provocation of others. Had it been deliberate, I would have got rid of him. He just was quite unaware of the presence and needs of other people—as if he had previously lived all alone, out in the desert, with no one to consider but himself. We put him in three-twelve because the suites on both sides are unoccupied."

"Had he any friends or relatives?" asked the priest.

"Hmmmmm. Offhand I would say no, but that, of course, is impossible. People must have friends—even people like Bodetkin, who lived, as it were, in outer space. Whether he got mail or not, I don't know. You'll have to check with Mrs. Frisbee at the desk. But he had no friends in the hotel, and I can never recall him receiving anyone in his rooms. But now you arouse my curiosity, Father. May I ask why you are interested in him?"

"I am not personally interested in him," said Father Bredder. "I am making inquiries on behalf of a friend of mine."

"The police?" asked Mr. Ambrose.

"Why do you think of the police?" countered the priest.

"Well, first of all because you have some reputation for being an investigator yourself, Father. And secondly, we have had a man here from the FBI inquiring about Mr. Bodetkin. And thirdly because a man as strange as Bodetkin, in my experience as a hotelier, is often the subject of police inquiries. You see, from my third reason, that I perhaps have a little talent for deduction myself."

"I am supposed to make my inquiries without arousing suspicion," said Father Bredder. "I am afraid I have failed."

"Father," said Mr. Ambrose, "forgive me if I make a personal remark. Whoever asked you to make discreet and unsuspected inquiries either did not know you very well or did not really expect you to do so. Guile and cunning are not in your nature. And you have done quite as well as the FBI man. He came on the pretext of checking on aliens living in the hotel. A routine check on reported residences. But everybody knew he was really interested in Bodetkin."

"How did they know?" asked the priest.

"Because everybody knows that Bodetkin worked in a plant involved in our national space effort. And he's dead. So there you are."

But this seemed to Father Bredder not a complete explanation, though he could not define the reasons for his doubts. He put the thought aside.

"Since I've failed to be subtle, I may as well be frank," he said. "Can I see Mr. Bodetkin's room?"

"Certainly," said Mr. Ambrose. "I'll give you the key. His possessions are as they were. He's only been dead three days, you know, and we are awaiting word on what to do with them."

"What's the usual procedure?"

"Put them in our storeroom for a while and then turn them over to the city authorities. They have a department that handles the unclaimed property of such people. I think the final disposition, if nobody turns up to claim it, is a public auction."

When he entered the room, Father Bredder found it so jumbled, with such a confusion of articles lying about, that all his hopes of making an inventory of its contents for Minardi were destroyed. There were stacks of books all over the living-room floor—books, sheet music for violin and piano, and records. There was a bookcase along one wall of the room in a similar disorder. Some of the books were upright on the shelves, others on their sides with records and sheet music piled on top of them or beside them. There were a number of unlabeled jars on the shelves containing chemicals, several rolls of audio tapes, and on a chair an expensive slide projector with an equally expensive 16-mm movie projector beside it.

He took out a handkerchief and rather self-consciously used it to open a cupboard so as not to leave fingerprints on the knob. The cupboard contained a complete photographic laboratory in miniature—developing and printing tanks, a drier, an enlarging camera, boxes of photographic paper and more shelves of chemicals.

Some negatives were hanging on a wire line, put there to dry. They were negatives of sheet music, showing the violin and piano score. Father Bredder had no musical training other than the painful piano lessons of boyhood. But examining the negatives, he could see that they were taken from a music manuscript—either an original composition or one which had been copied by hand and then photographed. He looked over all the negatives but could not find the title of the piece that had so interested Mr. Bodetkin. Some were scored in B-flat and others in D major. That much he knew from his boyhood struggles at the piano.

He went from the cupboard back to the living room and into the bedroom, and here again was the same jumble of books and music manuscripts and records. He was aware that there was something wrong with all this, and sat in a living-room chair to decide what it was.

"He liked photography, he liked music, he liked books," he said to himself, but aloud. "No. That is wrong. If he had really liked books and music, he would have kept his books and music in better order. Or would he?" He looked around at the disorder of the room. It suggested a search made among the sheet music and the books for some particular work.

He got up and examined the titles of some of the books. They showed a great diversity of subject matter. Cheiro's *Palmistry for All*, Vicker's *Mathematics for Modern Minds, In Search of Adam* by Wendt, *The Grapes of Wrath* by Steinbeck, *The Guns of August* by Tuchman, *Japan Subdued* by Feis and *Jack London, Sailor on Horseback* by Irving Stone. What was remarkable about the books was the lack of any one interest. The same proved true of the sheet music and the records. There were the Mendelssohn "Concerto in E Minor for Violin and Piano" and a record by the Beatles of their doleful songs.

There were an album of folk music by the Shaw Chorale, the original score of *Camelot,* a collection of sea chanties sung by Leonard Warren, and some nursery rhymes on a small 45-rpm record, and so on—a hodge-podge of records showing no particular musical leaning. The sheet music, however, was all classical and all for violin and piano. Much of it was old and dog-eared, and on top of one stack, indicating that it had been recently referred to, was a French edition of Corelli's *La Folia.* The edition was dated 1810, but if it had any value, Mr. Bodetkin was careless of it, for the sheets were torn and several of the pages had come away from the binding.

Father Bredder turned to the books again, for books were one of his great interests. He spent many hours and the few dollars that might be left over from his allowance in the secondhand bookstores, buying volumes that took his fancy—many of them properly neglected by the general public. Now, he was looking for one book which he reasoned, in so large and miscellaneous a collection, should be there. But he did not find it.

He was about to leave, confused by the disarray of the rooms, when he decided to pull the drapes which covered the window in the living room. He did so and gave a little cry of delight. Behind the drapes and outside the window was a box gay with petunias. They looked fresh and well-cared-for, and he opened the window and felt the mold in which they were growing. Then he closed it again and picked up the telephone.

"This is room three-twelve," he said. "Could you send the chambermaid up here?"

"Room three-twelve," said the operator, surprised.

"Yes. I would like to speak to the chambermaid."

A little later there was a knock on the door and a middle-aged woman, very thin and worried-looking, entered.

"You gave us all a start, sir," she said. "This was Mr. Bodetkin's room, and he's dead. Have you permission to be here?"

"Yes," said Father Bredder. "Mr. Ambrose gave me the key. Has anybody been in this room since Mr. Bodetkin died?"

"Yes. There was a man from the FBI here. And Mr. Ambrose was here."

"You yourself. Have you done any tidying?"

"Oh, no. Mr. Ambrose said the room was to be left. Nothing was to be touched."

"Did Mr. Bodetkin usually leave his room like this?"

The chambermaid glanced around. "Sometimes. But not very often. This is the worst I've seen it."

"Are you fond of flowers?" asked the priest.

"Flowers? Not especially."

"And you've done nothing in this room since Mr. Bodetkin died?"

Nothing at all. You can see that for yourself."

"Thank you," said Father Bredder.

When she had gone, he took one more look about, closed the drapes and then left, puzzled. He was puzzled about the one book that was missing from the random collection of Mr. Bodetkin. And he was puzzled by the fact that although Bodetkin had died three days before, the petunias in the window box had been watered that morning.

Four

for him.

LIEUTENANT MINARDI was a widower and a widower
with a not unusual problem, for he had a thirteen-year-
old daughter, Barbara, to bring up. He was himself a
Latin, for his birthplace was Sicily, and though his parents had migrated from Sicily when he was not yet in his
teens, he had absorbed into his nature some of the sto-
icism and melancholy of that grim, strong and beautiful
island.

He was a naturalized American but with European
roots, and there was a conflict or at least a separation
there. His past made him thoughtful and introspective
and gave to his character a touch of sadness. His present
demanded the brisk optimism of the American overlaid
with a kind of gay cynicism. This conflict, this grafting of
one growth upon another, was, of course, a problem
common to all immigrants to the United States, whatever
their background. Some tried to compensate by becoming more American than the Americans. Others, and
Minardi belonged to this group, rejected such a change
as false and honored his Sicilian past as fully as he
worked for his American present. He took from America
the things he enjoyed and accepted those aspects of the

country which did not appeal to him. He drew from Sicily a subtlety and a quietness and penetration of the motives of his fellow men which had much to do with his success as a police officer.

His daughter, Barbara Minardi, born in the United States, was fully American; and added to the complication of a father bringing up a daughter was the complication of a semi-European guiding an American. The lieutenant was at times quite lost in trying to handle her. He demanded of her a discipline and a respect not exacted by American parents. He had once spent two days deciding whether she could attend a teen-age dance and then he had taken her himself and had remained throughout the dance, to Barbara's disgust.

"You frighten off all the boys," she complained. "Who was going to dance with me with my father, a police officer, watching?"

"You're too young for dancing," said Minardi. "If you are going to dances at thirteen, what are you going to do for amusement when you are eighteen?"

"Go skiing in the Alps with one of those smooth Austrian ski bums," said Barbara, leaving her father incapable of replying.

Minardi lived in an apartment in Park La Brea Towers off Wilshire Boulevard. It was a modern apartment, fashionably furnished, but he had gentled it to his own personality with a few of the things that remained to him from his parents and some acquisitions of his own. He was fond of sculpture, anthropology, and history. Father Bredder was of the opinion that if Minardi had not become a policeman, he would have made a scholar of some eminence.

The day after his visit to the Porter Hotel, Father Bredder had been invited to dine with Minardi at his apartment and now, their dinner over, they sat in the living room before a picture window watching the light die out of the sky and the street lights emerge from the twilight, as if the world had been turned upside down and the stars of the heavens had become a carpet for the earth.

"Barbara will be back from Laguna this weekend," said Minardi. "And I have a week's vacation coming up. I've rented a little house in Avalon on Catalina for the week so she'll have something to do. I wonder whether you could join us?"

"Next Monday?" asked Father Bredder.

"Yes. But you could come over anytime. You know how Barbara enjoys your company. And there would be good fishing."

One reason for the invitation, Father Bredder knew, lay in the sentence, "You know how Barbara enjoys your company." The priest had become a sort of catalyst between father and daughter. When he was present, Minardi was relaxed with his daughter and they enjoyed each other more.

"I'd be glad to come," said the priest, "but I don't think I'll be able to make it until Wednesday. A builder is coming in to look over the air conditioning in the convent. Father Armstrong could handle it, but I need to know how it works myself, so I want to be there with the workmen. Also I may be able to keep them off my roses. But I can make it by Wednesday, for certain."

"Good. Barracuda and yellowtail are running according to the papers, and there may even be albacore. They're off San Diego now."

"Does Barbara like fishing?" asked the priest.

"Barbara? I don't know. She likes anything that's exciting."

"For some people fishing isn't exciting," said the priest. "But there'll be swimming and I think I've heard that there are horses to ride. Any of her friends coming with her?"

Minardi sighed. He never thought of things like that. "Thanks," he said. "I'll ask her if she wants to bring one or two along. The place has three bedrooms and sleeping room in the living room. So there'll be room." He was silent a moment, comtemplating the oddity that Father Bredder, who was celebate, was by nature a better father than he. "I'm too much wrapped up in myself," he said at length. "I never think in terms of company. The fault lies both in my nature and my calling."

"You are lonely and don't know it," said Father Bredder gently. "You should marry again. Barbara is thirteen now. Five or six more years and she will be gone from you. You have to face that."

"I've already thought of it," said Minardi. "When it happens, I'll face it."

"You'll face it," thought Father Bredder. "But you will be lonelier than ever—the worst kind of loneliness, for it will be unspoken."

"Let's talk of something else," said Minardi. "What happened at the Porter Hotel yesterday? Anything significant about Bodetkin?"

"Nothing that perhaps can't be explained in terms of

the peculiarities of human beings," said the priest. He described the variety of litter in Bodetkin's room, the wide range of the books and records and the photographic negatives he had seen in the darkroom. Minardi grunted.

"This is a sterile investigation," he said. "There's nothing to it. Bodetkin had a full security clearance, never aroused any suspicion, and died of a heart attack. That's it. I've seen some of the Federal reports. They've turned up nothing more on his background than what we knew all ready. Simmons from the FBI as much as admitted that as far as they are concerned, it is a necessary but routine investigation. I'll turn in my own report tomorrow and then my desk is cleared and I can enjoy Catalina."

Father Bredder hesitated. "Do you know anything about music?" he asked.

"Enough not to describe Tchaikovsky as a bridge between Beethoven and the moderns, as was done in the paper the other day."

"Do you know what is the relative minor key to D Major?"

"Hmmmmm," said Minardi. "Wait a minute. I have to make a sort of musical clock in my head and work it out. A minor."

"Which has three flats?"

"Yes. But what's all this about?"

"The photographic negatives of music manuscript in Bodetkin's room were in two keys," said the priest—"D major and B flat minor, which is not the relative for D major."

"So?" said the detective.

"Well, it's odd," said the priest. "Because if Bodetkin was photographing a musical composition, you wouldn't find two unrelated keys in it. I mean a composer doesn't just jump from one key to another unrelated key in the middle of the same piece without modulation."

"Maybe they were two separate compositions," said Minardi.

"On the same negative?" countered Father Bredder. "That's rather like photographing half a page of *A Tale of Two Cities* and half a page of . . . oh . . . the Baltimore *Catechism* in the same frame."

"What do you make of it?" asked the detective.

"It's just odd," said Father Bredder. "It suggests that the music was not photographed as music—for its musical content—but for some other reason."

"What other reason?"

"I don't know," said the priest.

"Anything else?"

"Well, there was the one missing book—the one book in that huge collection of books that I expected to see, but it wasn't there—at least as far as I could discover."

"What book?" asked Minardi.

"The Bible," said the priest.

"Oh, come now, Father," said the detective. "You mustn't let your vocation get in the way of your investigations. Lots of people own lots of books but never a Bible among them."

Father Bredder shook his head. "I don't believe it," he said. "When people buy books—even for status symbols—the Bible is among them. It's the world's most popular book, the full Testament, old and new. Maybe they never read it. But they have it. And yet in all that vast collection of all kinds of books in Bodetkin's suite there wasn't a Bible."

"What is the significance?" asked Minardi.

"I don't know," said the priest. "It's just odd."

"Not granted," said Minardi. "Your judgment is colored by your calling. Was there something else odd about the room?"

"Yes. There was a flower box outside Bodetkin's window in the living room, and the flowers had been watered that morning. They were petunias."

"Probably one of the hotel staff had instructions to water them daily."

"But the staff were forbidden to enter the room," said Father Bredder.

"Some people get into a routine of doing things and they think that such prohibitions don't apply to them," said Minardi. "If the flowers weren't watered by one of the hotel staff, who could have watered them?"

"I don't know," said Father Bredder. "It's just one of the oddities. Before I left the hotel, I checked with the manager and he said the flower box belonged to Bodetkin. There are none at any of the other windows. He received permission to put the flower box outside his window. So it was his flower box and his flowers. And he's dead. But someone continues to water them—even though, on police orders, no one is to enter the room."

"Hmmmmmmm," said Minardi. "Maybe there is something a little odd about that. And yet it may be just a matter of sentiment on the part of a friend."

"According to the manager, he had no close friends. And how could such a friend get into his room?"

Minardi shrugged. He really wasn't very interested. The most innocent acts or happenings, examined in isolation, became curious. That was one of the bugbears of his profession, and he had learned that only when there was an oddity in the whole picture was it worth investigating. His method was to get the over-all design complete in all its details and then start looking for flaws.

Father Bredder, on the other hand, didn't have a method. He operated by ear; by instinct. In his investigations he mixed up this world and the next as if they were all part of one and a holdup on Main Street had repercussions among the glittering hosts of Heaven. Once Minardi had pointed out to the priest that a policeman had to deal with the reality of the here and now—the world of tarmac and concrete and automobiles and living people. Father Bredder had replied, "That is not the reality. It is only a foreshadowing of the reality that lies beyond. In that sense, it is I who am the realist and you who deal with shadows."

"Explain," said Minardi.

"Well, how can anything be said to be real which has but a limited existence?" replied Father Bredder. "At best it is but an impression. Reality demands eternity. Without eternity there is no significance to anything."

"Well, the significance of a crime is that a law has been broken and it is the job of the police to discover who broke the law and punish him to discourage others."

"The significance of a crime is that a law of God, exemplified in the formation of society, has been broken and the crime remains until the offender repents," said Father Bredder. "The state will pass away. God will not."

Minardi reflected now on this view of the priest's. He himself was a detective employed by the Los Angeles Police Department. Father Bredder was a detective employed by God.

"All right, Father," he said gently. "Thank you for the pieces you have given me. I'll put everything together and turn in my report."

"There's one other thing I had forgotten about until this moment," said the priest. "Do you know of a Dr. Tighler?"

"Tighler?" said Minardi. "Tighler? Name seems familiar. Yes. There's a physicist called Tighler who used to work on the Atomic Energy Commission—or some job connected with AEC. He resigned after one of those Congressional loyalty checks. I forget the details if I ever knew them. I think that there was nothing against him except that his method of living made him a poor risk. He's a bachelor. About fifty, I'd think. But rather fond of women and high living and tending to indescretion."

"What kind of indiscretion?" asked the priest.

"Now you're asking me for details, and all I can give you is an impression. I think he had a cavalier attitude toward security precautions. Something comes to me now. Yes. At the inquiry he said that 'Confidential' in the security code meant something that all office boys knew, while 'Top Secret' was available to junior clerks but excluded office boys."

"Was that true?" asked Father Bredder.

Minardi hesitated before replying. "Some curious things happen in security in this country," he said. "I'll try to explain that with an example. Every now and then you see an item in the paper about some scientist leaving valuable papers in a taxi and losing them—sometimes not papers but dangerous drugs or something equally vital. Quite often, though the public doesn't know it, that's a plant. It's done to put people who might be after such papers off the trail for a day or two. Or to find out who might be after such things. Basically a frame-up.

"Sometimes it isn't. Sometimes somebody who ought to know a lot better gets careless with valuable and even vital material and leaves it lying about. It's hard to get Americans to be suspicious and remain suspicious. They're trusting by nature and forgiving, too. When we really got into this atomic energy and space stuff, the hardest job of security was to teach security to the people involved—real security, which means one hundred per cent suspicion of all others at all times.

"I fancy that Tighler was one of the people we couldn't teach security to. He figured it was all a child's game, and since he wouldn't take any other attitude, he was dropped from the inner circles, as it were. But why do you ask about him?"

"Because he called me to ask me to undertake an investigation for him he didn't want to turn over to the usual authorities," said the priest. "Is he still working on security matters?"

"No," said Minardi. "Private research now. Probably a grant from some organization. But he's got plenty of money of his own."

"He said it was a matter concerning national security," said the priest.

"It may have been," said Minardi. "What did you tell him?"

"I told him that since it wasn't a spiritual matter, I didn't feel I could help him. He was a little annoyed and said he would find someone else."

"I'd say that you gave him the proper answer," said Minardi. "Stick to your own calling. You might get into serious trouble if you get into the area that belongs to Intelligence."

After that they talked about baseball and the plight of the Los Angeles Dodgers, who had a strong pitching staff and not a real hitter on the whole roster.

Five

FATHER BREDDER had it in common with a great many of
his fellow men that he constantly forgot to return hotel
room keys. He didn't often stay at hotels, but when he
did, he could remember to return the key only if asked
for it by the cashier. He had not been a guest at the
Porter Hotel; he had received the key from the manager
and had left in such deep thought that he had neglected
to return it.

That was two days ago and, though Mr. Ambrose had
called him asking that the key be returned, he still had it
with him. So, when he left Minardi's apartment at ten
that evening, he decided to drop by the hotel and return
the key.

When he got to the Porter Hotel, however, it was
eleven at night and no desk clerk was on duty. There was
a slot in the front of the counter behind which the clerk
worked for returning keys, and he was about to slip the
key in there when he decided to take one more look at
Bodetkin's room. It was a spur-of-the-moment decision
and, before he knew the reasons he had made it, he was
already in the creaking self-service elevator and on his
way to the third floor. He stepped out into the corridor to

meet an oppressive quiet. The dim ceiling light did little to illuminate the hallway. There was a vaguely musty smell which the priest had not noticed in his previous visit and which brought the reflection that there was a lot to be said for air conditioning. The carpet was of the usual "hotel beige," and despite the dimness of the light, Father Bredder could see scars on the skirting board at the bottom of the walls of the corridor, made by several decades of carpet cleaners.

Walking down the corridor to Room 312, the priest noticed that there was no light coming from under any of the doors. The occupants were already either asleep or had not returned for the night. He understood the objection, in the quietness of the hotel, to the late Paul Bodetkin playing his recordings at this hour.

Room 312 would normally have been close to the elevator, but instead lay around a corner of the corridor, for the elevators of the hotel had been relocated and nobody had bothered to renumber the rooms. His feet made little noise as he walked, and in the silence he felt guilty, for he had no right to be visiting Bodetkin's room without the permission of the manger. He was sensitive about such scruples and asked himself why he was going to the room anyway. And the answer was a kind of instinct that he had missed something in his previous visit —some simple object or combination of objects that would give him the explanation of the jumble of books and records and music and photographs that made up the private life of Paul Bodetkin, who had formerly been a janitor at Interspace Technology in suburban Westchester. It was, after all, odd, he reflected, that a man who had occupied the lowly position of a janitor should have such a background—odd, anyway, for an American Janitor.

The name Bodetkin suggested foreign birth, though of course there were many native-born Americans with equally foreign or rather non-English-sounding names. The priest smiled. Some kind of inherited snobbery surely lay behind the thought that English-sounding names could be taken as American but foreign-sounding names were automatically thought of as foreign. Yet if Bodetkin had been foreign-born, he might have a taste for classical music or music of even a semi-classical nature as well as books. Not many native-born Americans at the janitor level had a taste for Prokofiev and Mendelssohn. And then he was abashed by the conclusion, for there was snobbery in that, too.

He was now approaching Bodetkin's room, and suddenly he stopped. He had seen an instant's gleam of light from under the door. He waited and the gleam appeared again and this time remained for a few seconds before disappearing.

For a moment the priest thought of slipping around the corner and watching to see who eventually came out of the room, for it was plainly occupied. But the disadvantage was that he almost certainly wouldn't be able to recognize the man in the dim light, and the corner was too far away, in any case, to be able to grab the intruder. The light at the bottom of the door reappeared and again disappeared.

The priest put his hand gently on the knob and tried to turn it. The door was locked. He took the key from his

· *49*

pocket, inserted it quickly in the lock, turned it and flung the door open, his nerves tingling. He switched on the lights by the side of the door, but they revealed an empty room. And then he found the explanation of the mystery and was mortified by the way he had allowed himself to be deceived. The light which he had seen appear and disappear under the door came from a flashing sign on a cinema across the street. The curtains of the living-room window were pulled apart and the light shone at intervals of a few seconds directly into the room and under the door.

He lowered his big frame onto a settee and considered the window. When he had last visited the room, in daylight, the heavy drapes had been drawn. That they were now pulled apart meant that somebody had been in the room since then, somebody who was either in a hurry or careless, for they had not drawn the drapes again.

Why had they moved the drapes at all? Obviously to do something at the window. He went to it and saw immediately what had been done. All the petunias had been uprooted and now lay wilted on the earth of the flower box.

"That's odd," he said to himself. "First somebody waters them after Bodetkin's death. And then somebody destroys them. Two completely opposite actions. A flower lover and, it would seem, a flower hater."

He wondered about this for a while, and intermixed with the subject of flowers came the thought of the books and the sheet music and the record collection and the photographs. He had the feeling, based on the scantiest of reasons, that the books had not been bought as books but for some other purpose, and the same was true of the sheet music and the record collection. And perhaps that was also true of the flowers. They were not there because Bodetkin loved flowers but for some other purpose. A signal? A notification to some other party that Bodetkin was occupying these rooms? In that case the destruction of the flowers would be a signal to whoever watched the room from the outside that Bodetkin was no longer occupying the tiny suite. But why then, Father Bredder asked himself, had someone watered the flowers after Bodetkin's death? And surely there were other and simpler ways of discovering whether Bodetkin was indeed occupying the rooms.

He started to examine the books again, picking up volume after volume and opening the pages and checking the binding and the dust jackets. Father Bredder was an expert on the look of a used book, for he bought all his own books at secondhand stores. He could judge with reasonable accuracy the amount of use a book had had. The first item to show any sign of wear was the dust jacket at the top and bottom of the spine. Little tears or cracks in the paper appeared here if a book had been taken off a shelf as much as three or four times.

All the books he examined had these little telltale tears. And yet there was something strange about them. None had the appearance of having been read through from cover to cover—a process which, in the priest's experience, made the book slightly lopsided in its binding unless binding and paper were of the highest quality. He continued his examination. Every book had been looked at, used, but none appeared to have been read from cover to cover.

He remembered the darkroom in the cupboard and

went into it. The negative photgraphs of music that had been hanging there to dry were gone.

He remained in the room for over an hour, puttering around among the books and music. When he left, he was aware only that there was some spiritual conflict about the place—a lack of harmony which deeply disturbed him. Reaching the lobby, he slipped the key into the slot in the front of the desk clerk's counter and then returned to the convent.

When he reached his room, he found a note in Father Armstrong's handwriting. It read: "Call Lieutenant Minardi when you get in." The number given to call was not Minardi's home but a Crestview number that seemed familiar. Father Bredder glanced at his watch. It was, to his horror, one in the morning. He made the call, and Minardi answered immediately.

"Tighler's dead," he said. "Did you have an appointment to see him this evening—after leaving me?"

"No," said the priest. "Not at all. Why?"

"Well, there was a note in his pocket saying he had an appointment to see you at eleven P.M. You are quite sure that you didn't have such an appointment but forgot about it?"

"Quite sure," said Father Bredder.

"According to his housekeeper, a priest was with him just before he died. The priest left and the housekeeper came in to see if Tighler needed anything further and found him dead in his chair. That was about eleven-thirty P.M. Have you any witnesses to account for the places you have been between now and when you left me?"

"No," said the priest. "None at all. Actually I was in

the Porter Hotel, visiting Bodetkin's rooms. Nobody saw me there."

Minardi sighed. "You know, Father," he said, "you have the most astonishing gift for getting yourself into trouble. I'm at Tighler's place now. Simms won't commit himself without an autopsy, but it looks like murder. And according to the housekeeper, a priest called Father Bredder was with Tighler just before he died or was murdered."

"Do you want me to come over to answer some questions or make a statement?" asked Father Bredder.

Minardi hesitated before replying. "That's what I should ask you to do," he said, "but it will wait until morning in your case."

"Thank you," said Father Bredder. "I'm a little tired and need a good night's rest."

"Good luck," said Minardi and hung up.

Six

"WELL, IT'S MURDER," said Minardi sadly. "Murder by a man who looked like you and said he was you when he was admitted by the housekeeper. And I wish to goodness that you hadn't been roaming around in Bodetkin's room but had gone back to your own quarters and to bed—having awakened someone first to establish that you were home."

"Do you have to arrest me?" asked Father Bredder.

"If I didn't know you, I would," said Minardi. "On suspicion. But I won't."

"Well, you must do your duty," said the priest. "Father Armstrong could handle the air conditioning."

"What air conditioning?"

"The men who are coming to put in air conditioning in the classrooms."

Minardi fished a cigarette out of a pack, broke off the filter tip, put the cigarette in his mouth, lit it, and inhaled deeply. "Doesn't anything ever bother you, Father?" he asked, the inhaled smoke coming out with the words.

"Yes," said the priest. "The roses. We've had them three years now and they have a good root system. And Bodetkin's room. There's something the matter with the things in it. There's something wrong there—spritually."

"I mean doesn't it bother you that Tighler has been murdered and we have evidence to show that you had an appointment with him just before he was murdered and a witness who is prepared to testify that you or someone remarkably like you was with him a few minutes before he was found dead in his chair?"

"No," said the priest. "Because it wasn't me."

"But you haven't got an alibi," said the detective, exasperated.

The priest nodded in simple agreement. "How was he killed?" he asked.

"He was suffocated. We don't know how. There are a few bruises on the body, but they're comparatively slight. Simms thinks that the murderer somehow managed to get Tighler between two mattresses or something of the sort, pinned him there and then held a hand over his mouth and nose until he died. There's a big sofa in the room that would serve, I suppose. But the thing is physically impossible, apart from the strength involved. The odd thing is that there isn't a bruise or a scratch on Tighler's nose or mouth. You'd think he would have been able to struggle enough to be bruised. Simms is examining Tighler's hands and nails for traces of skin or hair or fabric or anything that could give us a clue to his assailant. He must have put up a fight. Good Heavens. You just don't let someone suffocate you without a tremendous struggle."

"Could he have been unconscious before he was suffocated?" asked the priest.

"Possibly," said Minardi. "But Simms will be able to

tell us about that later. Who knew that Tighler had called you a few days ago?"

"As far as I know, only Father Armstrong. He gave me the message."

"And you refused to see Tighler?"

"Yes."

"Did you discuss that decision with Father Armstrong?"

"Yes."

"And what did he say?"

"He said I ought to have gone to see him," said the priest. "I think he was right," he added dejectedly. "He very often is."

"Well," said Minardi. "If you don't mind, I'll take you up to Tighler's place and confront you with the housekeeper and see whether she recognizes you. She said she got a good look at the man who said he was you and wouldn't fail to recognize him again."

"Good," said Father Bredder. "I certainly think that I ought to go up there. I have a suggestion to make about the housekeeper."

"What is it?" asked Minardi.

"Don't ask her in my presence whether she recognizes me as the man who came to the house to see Tighler just before he died."

"Why?" asked Minardi. "You have a right to be present when I put that question."

"She might be reluctant to answer truthfully," said the priest. "Out of respect for my calling. It is very important at this stage to get a completely truthful answer from her."

56 ·

Minardi grunted. "Okay," he said.

They took the Hollywood Freeway westward to its intersection with Sunset Boulevard and then continued west along Sunset to North Canyon Drive. On the freeway and on Sunset Boulevard itself the glare of the sun was worse even than the heat. A slight misting of smog extended several hundred feet up into the air, and this served not only to increase the glare and the heat but to irritate the eyes to the point of smarting.

Everything—the cars, the houses of Spanish style to the sides of the freeway, the streets below and even the nonproductive king palms—had a harshness and stridency that irritated the nerves, and Father Bredder was glad when the car turned into North Canyon Drive and started snaking up the tarmac road, shaded from the sun by bowers of trees, all foreign to this desert area and all plenteously watered.

Dr. Tighler's house was one of the older residences in this fashionable and expensive area of West Los Angeles. It was built of stucco, exquisitely whitewashed and very handsome under its red pantile roof. There was a driveway of perhaps a hundred yards and then a delicate wrought-iron gate through the stucco walls that surrounded the house. An arch lay over the gate, and this was embowered with bougainvillea, still blooming in scarlet profusion.

Inside the gate was a courtyard of red house bricks— an expansive area sufficient to contain a dozen or more cars, and in the center of this courtyard was a fountain with the inevitable lightly clad maiden pouring water out of a ewer. Broad and low brick steps led from the courtyard to a terrace before the house. The terrace was covered over with unroofed rafters, and strewn across these to provide a roof was more bougainvillea mixed with a large honeysuckle vine, the plants growing up the pillars that supported the rafters.

The doorway was huge and there were tiles with a blue design set into the stucco walls around the doorway. Father Bredder recognized them at a glance as azulejos—the handmade tiles of Portugal—for he had been to Portugal and had seen many of them there. It was a little surprising to find these tiles in Los Angeles, for they were not plentifully imported.

They were admitted by the housekeeper, who gave a little start when she saw Father Bredder, her hand going halfway to her mouth as if she were going to stifle a cry.

"Good afternoon," said the priest. "Could you take us to Dr. Tighler's study?" He had agreed to make this little address so that the housekeeper would be able to compare his voice with that of the previous visitor who had said he was Father Bredder.

The woman looked confused, and Father Bredder had to repeat the question before, without replying, she turned and led them down a quiet corridor, past a broad flight of carpeted stairs, to a room in the rear.

"Go in, Father," said Minardi, opening the door. "I'll be with you in a while." The study was large enough to have provided the living room of an ample house. There was an expansive window along the wall with a view beyond it of a small terrace and, below that, a slope of garden with a swimming pool at the bottom.

There was a high fence all around the garden, draped with plumbago, snail vine and thick growths of red and white ivy geraniums. The living fence provided complete privacy for anyone using the swimming pool. The wall to the right of the window was painted a moss green, and there were two white doors in it. Father Bredder opened them both and found one leading to a bathroom and the other to a bedroom. There was no connecting door between bedroom and bathroom, so this was obviously not the original use of these two rooms. The other two walls of the study were taken up with bookshelves.

The study was carpeted in a deep pile gray carpet, fairly new, and there were comfortable cretonne-covered chairs grouped around a large coffee table in the center of the room. Along the bottom of the wall in which the two doors lead to the bathroom and the bedroom was an ample settee and over it a large picture which could have been an impressionist's rendering of a yachting regatta or a stained-glass window, depending on what the observer rather than the painter had in mind. The canvas was edged with a light white wooden frame which came down to within a foot of the back of the settee.

The priest sat on the settee for a moment and found it to be one of those pieces of furniture which embraced rather than supported the sitter. He sank so deeply into it that he had a little difficulty getting to his feet again. He backed to the center of the big study to look at the picture, trying to decide whether the artist had intended a yachting regatta or a stained-glass window. It was the sort of picture that might appear in a magazine supplement of a Sunday newspaper—a supplement devoted to interior decorating. In short, the picture was a piece of design rather than a piece of art, and curious as to the artist, the priest looked at the lower corners of the canvas and found there only an ill-formed letter T.

From the picture he turned to examine the books. Those in the bookcase on one wall were all scientific volumes. The greater part of them were leather-bound collections of papers by different researchers identified only by the author. He took down one at random. On the spine was the name Pickton and nothing more. Inside was a printed thesis with the title *Some Characteristics of Super-sonic Vibrations in the Medium Elements.* Another was titled *Report on Series A Experiments on Ultra-violet Emissions of Amorphous Carbons.*

Baffled by such heavy fare, the priest turned to the other bookcase. Here the taste in reading was wide—popular novels and biographies, detective stories, books of light verse, popular histories of the Civil War and so on. There was no particular kind of book dominant, and many of the titles were books which had not had any widespread appeal, though some had been best sellers.

He looked the books over carefully and found several titles which belonged in Bodetkin's collection. The book by Feis, *Japan Subdued,* and Vickers, *Mathematics for Modern Minds,* and Stone's, *Jack London, Sailor on Horseback.* Was there something odd about that—a janitor and a scientist with a similar taste in reading? The Stone book had been a best seller in its day, but the Feis book was hardly popular fare. And yet it might be just a coincidence. He looked about the study but found no radio phonograph, no records, and no sheet music.

"Well, it's odd," he reflected, thinking of the titles both had possessed. "But it may mean nothing." He continued with his examination of the titles and was deeply engrossed in this when Minardi came in, and with him, the housekeeper. The detective was worried.

"Mrs. Hanker says she is prepared to identify you as the man who called on Dr. Tighler just before he was murdered," he said. "Maybe you want to question her."

"That's kind of you," said the priest and turned to the housekeeper. "Don't be nervous," he said. "You must say what you believe to be the truth. Sit down. I know this must have been a big trial to you. But if you will answer me some questions, perhaps we can find out who it was who killed him."

"You killed him," said the woman. "It was you. Nobody else was with him but you." Her voice was both frightened and defiant.

"It is natural for you to believe so," said the priest. "But that is not what I wanted to ask you about. I wanted to ask you about Dr. Tighler's books."

"His books?"

"Yes. Do you know where he bought them?"

"The Pickwick Bookstore. In Hollywood."

"Did he go there himself and pick them out?"

"Yes. But sometimes he had them delivered."

"Did he often sit up late at night?"

"I think so. I can't say for certain. I went to bed myself at ten every evening normally. Dr. Tighler was very considerate about that."

"When you think he sat up, do you think he was reading?"

"Yes. I know he was reading because the books he was reading were usually left out of the shelves."

"What books were they?"

"I didn't look at the titles."

"Well, were they his scientific books or those others?"

"Mostly the others."

"Now, last night when you say I called on Dr. Tighler, did Dr. Tighler tell you he was expecting me?"

"No."

"At what time did this person call?"

"About eleven. A little before eleven."

"But you normally go to bed at ten. Why were you up?"

"I was doing some mending in my room. It is near the front of the house. I heard the doorbell and, since I had not undressed, I answered it."

"And what did the caller say?"

The woman hesitated. "I've told that to the police," she said. "I don't have to answer again, do I?" The question was addressed to Minardi.

"That's quite all right," said Father Bredder. "I hadn't intended to ask that question, but only to talk about the books and other things. Was Dr. Tighler fond of music?"

"I can't say."

"He has no radio phonograph?"

"He has a radio in his bedroom. And there's one in the living room."

"Does either play records?"

"No."

"He never played phonograph records?"

"No."

"He didn't play a musical instrument?"

"No."

"Was Dr. Tighler fond of flowers?"

"No. No more than anybody else."

"He didn't do any gardening himself?"

"No."

"Thank you very much," said the priest. He turned to Minardi. "I think the next move is up to you," he said gently.

Seven

"I WANT YOU to go ahead and take your vacation," said Captain Redwood. "I'll handle the Tighler case myself in your absence. Enjoy yourself on Catalina. Great time of the year to be there. I hear they've caught a few swordfish and the albacore are coming in."

Captain Redwood was Minardi's superior in Homicide. A square block of a man, practical, unimaginative and unemotional, he lived in Altadena and, for a policeman, took a surprising interest in community affairs in his home town. He belonged to the Chamber of Commerce, the City Planning Commission, and the local Rotary Club. He liked his community, refused to hold himself, because of his position, aloof from its affairs, and indeed found the meetings of the Chamber of Commerce and the Wednesday Rotary luncheons a relief from the violent world of his professional activity.

"A man should try to live as normal a life as he can," he once told Minardi. "The normal man is the support of his whole community. He doesn't get into trouble, pays his bills, helps to get the roads paved and the street lighting improved, and the school bonds passed. That's the proper way to spend a life."

Because of his philosophy, he was known among his juniors as Normal Redwood. He had been thirty years with the Los Angles police department, reported to work punctually at nine in the morning, took precisely one hour for lunch (except on Wednesdays when he went to the Rotary luncheon) and left precisely at five in the evening. He used police cars only on police work and drove to and from his work in a black Ford convertible which was twelve years old and was kept in excellent mechanical condition. Captain Redwood did the work on it himself, though he was entitled to have the car overhauled in the extensive police garage.

Minardi didn't want to take his vacation, however. He was tired. That was true because before the Tighler case came up, he had been working on another case which had involved extensive travel to Mexico. It was also true that Barbara would be looking forward to the holiday, and this was really the only chance he had to spend some uninterrupted time with her. But apart from those considerations, he hated to leave a case unsolved; his friend Father Bredder had become enmeshed in the Tighler affair, and so he had a personal as well as a professional interest in it. Perhaps, he reflected, that was one reason why Redwood was insisting on his taking the holiday anyway.

"I'd sooner delay the vacation a week or so," said Minardi. "There are some aspects of this case that are hard to pin down but need thinking about and looking into."

"Can't be done," said Redwood. "That would upset the department vacation schedule. Hazelwood and Judding are due to take their vacations immediately after you return. In any case, I don't like departures from the normal. This department has to be able to function like any other business. You know I have always held that no one man was essential to any one case."

"All right," said Minardi. "You have the whole file on your desk there up to date. I've suggested a couple of lines of investigation that I think might be most fruitful. There isn't much more I can say."

To himself, he added, "If he wants me to bring up Father Bredder, he's going to be disappointed. He can bring the subject up himself."

Captain Redwood did. "About Father Bredder," he said. "We've got the housekeeper's sworn statement that he was with Tighler before Tighler died. She identified him, with you as a witness, as the man who called on Tighler. From what we know of Tighler's murder, he was suffocated by a very powerful man. Father Bredder is a very powerful man. What are your views on all this?"

"I've put them down there in that report," said Minardi. "I think it's a case of either mistaken identity or deliberate false evidence. I am quite sure that Father Bredder is not guilty of the murder."

"He's a friend of yours, isn't he?" asked Redwood.

"Yes, he is."

"That would color your judgment a bit."

"Yes," said Minardi calmly. "It would. It's bound to. But I've known Father Bredder for fifteen years, and he couldn't kill a fly—let alone murder a fellow human being. That isn't prejudice. It's knowledge of the individual man."

"Most murders are done by people who seem completely innocuous," said Redwood.

"Yes," said Minardi. "But in each case there is overwhelming motive for killing. In Father Bredder's case, there isn't a trace of a motive."

"There's the telephone call from Tighler," said Redwood. "There's a link between the two of them there. We have only Father Bredder's statement of what actually happened during that telephone call."

"He says Father Armstrong was listening to his end of the conversation," said Minardi. "I'd intended questioning him as my next step."

"And there's one other link," said Redwood. "Bodetkin."

"Bodetkin? He's outside of the case altogether."

"Not quite," said Redwood. "There's a link between Bodetkin and Tighler. You've overlooked it."

"What link?" asked Minardi.

"Father Bredder," said the other. "That would have been perfectly obvious to you if you hadn't been a close personal friend of the priest's. Father Bredder got a telephone call from Tighler. And Father Bredder became very curious about Bodetkin."

"He was curious about Bodetkin because I asked him to make some inquiries for me," said Minardi. "It's all in that report you have there. I asked him to make the inquiries because people are more at ease with a priest than they are with a police officer who is making an investigation."

"Agreed," said Redwood. "But you told him that the case on Bodetkin was closed; that there was no need for further inquiry. And immediately after you told him that, he says he went to Bodetkin's room and spent a couple of hours there."

"Look," said Minardi. "If he went to Bodetkin's room and spent a couple of hours there, he couldn't possibly have murdered Tighler."

"That's the trouble with these personal friendships in police work," said Redwood. "They are hard to avoid because we are all human. But they are always damaging. In your case, your friendship with Father Bredder has blinded you to some pretty obvious possibilities. Father Bredder left your apartment at Park La Brea Towers about ten-thirty. Park La Brea Towers is not too far from North Canyon Drive. He could have got to Bodetkin's rooms at the Porter Hotel to remove some kind of evidence connecting Bodetkin and Tighler and providing a clue to the motive for the murder. Physically, considering the time element, that was possible. And anything that was possible must be gone into. Particularly since this priest took such an uncommon interest in Bodetkin."

"At my instigation," said Minardi.

"At your instigation in the first instance," said Captain Redwood. "But that second search of the rooms was entirely on his own volition. He had a pretty strong motive for that second search."

"All right," said Minardi. "But why would he tell me he had made the search if it was made for some secret purpose?"

"Because he wanted to avoid any risk of your finding out on your own account," said Redwood. "There was always the possibility that he was seen entering the hotel or in the hotel. By the way, how did he get to your place?"

"He rode the bus."

"Well, there's no bus up to North Canyon Drive. He must have taken a taxi up there. How did the house-keeper say that the man who called on Tighler arrived?"

"By car."

"Father Bredder has a car?"

"No."

"He could borrow one?"

"Everybody can borrow a car. But he'd have a hard time borrowing one around my neighborhood."

"You are forgetting that he may not have come to your apartment by bus at all. He may have come in a borrowed car and left it a little distance away."

Minardi was not often angry, but he began now to feel irritated. He was nervously tired after many months of work, and he resented his failings in the case being pointed out to him by Redwood as if he were a mere rookie. He fought the irritation down with some effort and tried to make another person out of himself—to become not Minardi, friend of Father Bredder, but merely a homicide detective who was a friend to nobody, including his own chief. In that role he began to see that the points Redwood was making had some validity.

"Father Bredder said that he was interested in Bodet-kin because there were some unnormal or abnormal elements in his room," he said. "There were, in his view, books that were not used as books and music that was not used as music. He has shown a unique sensitivity in this area during my experience with him. That sort of thing bothers him. His approach has worked well in the past.

"In questioning the housekeeper at Tighler's, he wasn't much concerned with shaking her identification of him. He was concerned with the same things that struck him about Bodetkin. That is to say, books and music. I am telling you this because they are elements—important elements—in the case as far as he is involved. If he is guilty, the clue to his guilt may lie in his interest in these elements."

For a while Redwood said nothing. He was seated in a swivel chair before his desk with a large window behind him. He turned around in his chair, so as to partly face the window, and looked out at the Federal Building opposite and the tip of a king palm baking in the smog and sunlight which he could just see between the two buildings. He hated the palm. It was supported by guy wire. Cut any of the guy wires and the palm would fall down. It was an artificiality as the smog was an artificiality. Neither was normal, and he liked normal things.

"Okay," he said, turning around again. "You're beginning to think like a detective again. There's something valuable there." He picked up the telephone and asked for the legal department. "Redwood here," he said. "Do whatever is necessary for us to get possession of all the effects of Paul Bodetkin, deceased, at the Porter Hotel. Yes. I'll fill out the form. No. We won't need to bring them here. I just want to keep them where they are and out of the hands of the public receiver.

"And while you are at it, I want the same thing done

with all Tighler's effects at his home. I want whatever legal steps taken that are necessary to ensure that nobody removes a single item from Tighler's house. And whatever warrants we require to enter either of these premises at will. Make sure it's all legal and the i's are dotted and the t's crossed." He put down the receiver and turned to Minardi.

"The way the courts are handling cases these days, the whole traditional process of police investigation tends to become illegal," he said. "If my hunch is right," he said, "there is something a lot bigger in this than the death of Bodetkin and the murder of Tighler. Don't let us forget that Bodetkin, though only a janitor, was working in a top security plant. And Tighler had been dropped from government employ as a securities risk."

"And the only link we have between the two is a Roman Catholic priest whose two major interests in life are children and gardening," said Minardi. "Are you going to arrest him?"

"Not yet," said Redwood. "But we'll keep a watch on him."

"That should be easy," said Minardi. "He's coming to Catalina with me to do some fishing and help entertain my daughter. Of course, since I'm on vacation, you will have to assign someone else to tailing Father Bredder."

Redwood gave him a hard look. "That will be all," he said, and concluded the interview.

Eight

SANTA CATALINA ISLAND, the holiday island for Los
Angeles, San Pedro and all the scattered communities of
the coastline between, managed to retain its air of en-
chantment despite the overcrowding of the tiny town of
Avalon with holiday makers. The streets of that toy city,
though thronged with visitors in huge straw hats and
shortened shorts, still held a dreamy loveliness and leisure, and it seemed to Father Bredder that the city had
enchanted the crowds rather than the crowds disenchant-
ing the city.

The palms on the street fronting the beach looked as
though they belonged there. The brick planters fronting
the ocean were gay with blossoms and the water positively
cerulean. There was little bad-tempered shouting or
bickering among the holiday makers who strolled rather
than walked along the pavements and down the middle
of the roads, unworried by heavy automobile traffic, for
the number of cars in Avalon was limited. The cars
deferred to the people rather than the people to the cars,
and Father Bredder reflected that perhaps this was one of
the factors which gave Avalon, though overcrowded, its
special air of ease and pleasure. Man, for once, was
superior to his own machinery.

The priest had been met as he came down the gangplank of the island steamer by Barbara Minardi and her father. Barbara had, as a gift of welcome, thrust into his hand a stick with a huge cloud of pink cotton candy on it. And then she had exclaimed for all around to hear, "Gosh, Father. You aren't even in uniform." Father Bredder had decided to spend his short holiday on Catalina in lay clothing, and wore a monstrous blue silk shirt, splotched with a design of islands and palm trees, and a pair of light pants—the shirt being the gift of the nuns at the Convent of Holy Innocents, who were inclined to be mischievous in such matters.

"Golly! If Reverend Mother could see you now," said Barbara, "she would have a fit."

"She's already seen me," said the priest, nibbling with pleasure at the cotton candy, for it was several decades since he had eaten such stuff. "I had to show the nuns what it looked like."

"What did they say?" demanded Barbara.

"They said I was to be careful not to lose the buttons because they are a special kind."

"That comes of being a nun, I suppose," said Barabara. "I think you look drooly. Doesn't he?"

Minardi nodded. Drooly was not the word he would have picked, but the big priest in the boldly designed shirt certainly looked imposing.

"We've got a real keen place," said Barbara. "You can walk right into the living room in your bare feet, and there's an outside shower and a Frosty Freeze on the corner, and it's all painted up in blue and orange."

It turned out that it was the living room and not the Frosty Freeze that was painted blue and orange. There was dark blue linoleum on the floor, and the furniture was painted a bright orange, but the walls, mercifully, were a neutral shade. The bungalow, called "The Mizzentop," lay toward the rear of the town, on an unpaved road with bright oleander hedges on each side. Each house on the street displayed its own gay candy-striped awnings, and many of them had sleeping porches in the front.

Father Bredder arrived at eleven in the morning, and Barbara insisted they have lunch at a place where they served "yard-long hot dogs" with some sweet relish which she said was dreamy, and then go for a swim.

"I'm glad you're here," said Minardi. "I've been eating yard-long hot dogs for two days. Maybe you can spell me. I'm going to get a hamburger next door." The hot dog place was crowded, but Barbara waited to be served by a tall, freckled boy with wiry hair and a snub nose and a paper for-and-aft cap on his head on which was written in red the word "Rick." He gave her extra relish and a smile. Later, after the swim, while Barbara was still in the water, the priest and Minardi sat in the shade of one of the desert palms growing on the beach.

"Barbara hasn't a friend with her?" asked the priest.

"No," said Minardi. "Her girl friend couldn't come. She got mumps or measles or something."

"Well, I think she has a boy friend," said the priest.

"A boy friend?" exclaimed Minardi. "She's only a child."

"Fourteeen, I think," said the priest. "That isn't a child these days. His name is Rick and he's the one with the freckles who serves those huge hot dogs."

"Well, I'll be hanged," said Minardi. "How did you know?"

"Oh," said the priest. "When I was a kid, I used to work in a drugstore, and there was a girl who came in every day for a soda from me. Something about the way those two looked at each other reminded me of that girl. In fact, I've never forgotten her. Didn't something of the sort occur when you were a teen-ager?"

"No," said Minardi. "My parents were strict. There wasn't any mixing of boys and girls. And no drugstores or hot dog places. Money mattered, and work. And Sunday Mass and evening Benediction and Confessions on Saturday. And not much else."

Father Bredder's face was sad as he ran his hand through the cool sand. "That's a pity," he said. "There has to be room for just being young. If God hadn't intended us to be young, we would all have been born thirty years of age or so. We're supposed to be happy here." He looked at the sparkling beauty of the bay, at the cliffs of the woodland to the right of them, strong and capped on the tops with the blaze of the sunshine. The sand in his hand felt clean and good, and all this splendor was the gift of the Creator and its enjoyment part of the worship of God, and so sea and sun and cool clean sand were related to Church and Mass and Benediction and Vespers—an intermingling and not a separation.

"It's all so simple," he said half aloud. "It's only when people separate the two that everything becomes a problem."

"Huh?" asked Minardi.

"I was talking to myself," said the priest. "About

things that are so simple that I can't even explain them. Maybe that's why there is music. Words just aren't up to the job."

"Talking about music," said Minardi. "Barbara wants to go to the dance at the Pavilion tonight. And there's enough loose kids around this island to stock Juvenile Hall."

"Who with?"

"She just said 'friends.' "

"Hmmmmm," said Father Bredder. "Well, she should have fun."

"She doesn't go unless I know who she's going with," said Minardi grimly.

"I fancy you will," said Father Bredder.

There were two landing piers in Avalon Bay. At one of them, the bigger, the island steamer docked and off-loaded or filled up with passengers. The other was a pier for pleasure craft, of which there were perhaps a hundred on moorings in the pellucid water. Toward the end of this pier was the Harbor Masters office, and Father Bredder suggested that they take a stroll over to it and watch some of the small sloops and powerboats coming alongside. But Minardi wanted to doze on the sand, so the priest went off alone on the exploration of this pier.

It held many fascinations for him. There was a weather station on one side with a circular indicator which showed the exact speed and direction of the wind at any moment, gave the state of the tide, the temperature and humidity. There was an aquarium of salt-water fish found off the island, including the splendid red-gold garibaldis and the lovely but tiny blue and gold Catalina

76 ·

gobies. There were a small octopus and several lobsters and a moray eel in the aquarium, and all these creatures interested the priest; particularly the moray eel which, with its spatulate head, blue eyes and fierce mouth, which it kept opening and shutting, seemed the quintessence of savagery. The priest looked at the fierce head of the eel and felt sorry for it. To look so fierce was to be taken as fierce, yet the eel only obeyed the laws of living laid down by its creator.

While watching the eel, he saw in the reflection on the glass of the aquarium a man standing slightly to the rear of him. He was a big, heavy man in his mid-thirties, muscular and clad in tan slacks and a white T-shirt. His hair was cropped short and showed signs of thinning on top. He seemed familiar. Father Bredder recalled that the man had been on the steamer with him coming over, and he had also seen him nearby on the beach while he was talking to Minardi. He had the impression that he had also seen the man somewhere else, but could not recall the occasion to mind.

Father Bredder passed on from the examination of the aquarium to a landing stage for small craft on the right-hand side of the pier. He arrived there in time to see a small blue-hulled powerboat come alongside with two scuba divers aboard, one at the wheel. They were clad in their glistening black neoprene wetsuits and, anxious to make the acquaintance of such interesting people, Father Bredder took the line that one threw to him as the launch neared the jetty and belayed it on a cleat. Lying in the spacious cockpit of the launch (the boat was almost all cockpit, there being only a small cuddy of a cabin forward) were two large silver fish, perhaps five feet in length.

"What are they?" he asked.

"White sea bass," said one of the men. "Got them off the point this morning." At that moment the other man, who had been at the steering wheel, turned around and Father Bredder glanced in surprise from one to the other.

"You're twins," he exclaimed.

"That's right," said the first of them. "My name's Bill Meistrell, and this is my brother Bob."

"I'm Father Bredder."

"I knew that," said Bill. "I've seen your picture in the papers. What are you doing over here? Somebody been shot?"

"No," said the priest. "I'm just on a vacation."

"We ought to get those fish out of the sun," said Bob.

"I know it," said Bill. "Quit worrying."

He went down into the little cuddy and emerged with several burlap sacks. He threw the sacks over the fish, plunged a bucket on a line into the ocean, and threw several bucketfuls of water over the sacks.

"That'll hold them," he said. "I want to get out of this wetsuit. I'm beginning to itch."

"We can't leave the *Linda Kay* here," said Bob.

"Quit fussing," said Bill, "or you'll be sixty before I'm forty. I'm going ashore to get a Coke, and then we can come back and take her to a mooring. Stick around, Father, if you've got nothing to do, and come have a Coke with us."

He went down into the cuddy and in a remarkably short while appeared dressed in work pants and a T-shirt.

His twin brother Bob did the same and, seeing them close together, the priest noted that Bill had a slight scar on his right eyebrow. Otherwise their features were almost identical, round, cheerful and frank, though Bill seemed the more solemn of the two, or perhaps serious was the word.

Stepping off the launch, Bob turned to a youngster among the crowd that had gathered to see the divers and the fish they had speared. "How about keeping an eye on the boat for us," he said. "Won't be long."

" 'Dive 'N Surf Marine Photography,' " said the youngster, reading the lettering on the side. "Do you make those diving movies for TV like *Sea Hunt?*"

"No. We inspect pipelines," said Bob. "How about it? Will you watch the boat?"

"Okay. But you got to give me a ride when you come back."

"Okay," said Bob, and they set off down the pier for a drugstore and soda fountain. Neither of the twins topped five foot eight, so Father Bredder towered over them, but they were very fast walkers and he had to make an extra effort to keep up with them.

"I'm going to eat," said Bill when they were seated in the cafe part of the drugstore. A waitress appeared and, without looking at the menu, he said, "Give me a hamburger and some French fries."

"I can hardly believe it," said Bob. "You come here for a Coke and order lunch." He turned to the waitress. "I'll take the same," he said.

"Just coffee for me," said Father Bredder.

"Last time I heard anything about you, Father," said

Bob, "was when you found the piece of that diver fishing off the Hermosa Beach Pier."

"Did they ever find out anything more about him?" asked Father Bredder.

"Nothing wrong with his gear," said Bob. "Our shop is in Hermosa Beach and, when there are diving accidents, the police bring the gear round to us. It checked out swell. There was even air in the tank. And the regulator was working."

"After all that time on the bottom?" said Father Bredder, surprised.

"Yeah. The hoses were gone, but the regulator itself worked. We put new hoses on it and Bill tried it out in the pool. Worked swell. It was a good regulator. Pretty new."

"If his equipment was working and he had air in his tank, how did he die?"

"Pass the ketchup," said Bill, and Bob did so. Bill judiciously poured some ketchup on his French fries, and Bob did precisely the same.

"You've heard of bends?" asked Bill.

"It wasn't bends," said Bob.

"I know it wasn't bends," said Bill. "I just asked Father whether he had heard of bends, that's all."

"You're just going to confuse him," said Bob.

"Will you keep quiet," said Bill. "You'll wind up confusing me."

"I've heard of bends," said Father Bredder.

"That's what I mean," said Bill. "Everybody's heard of bends. Every diver that dies, the papers say he got bends. Actually, hardly anybody dies of bends. Because anybody who knows about diving, knows enough to watch out for them. And anyway, there's a decompression chamber, and bends don't kill right away, so you can usually get to a decompression chamber when the symptoms appear and get decompressed."

"Brother, if that wouldn't confuse anybody, I don't know what would," said Bob.

"Will you be quiet?" said Bill. "Let me handle this in my own way. I just want Father to understand that it wasn't bends and get all idea of bends out of his mind."

"I remember it was some other thing, but I've forgotten what," said the priest.

"Air embolism," said Bill. "Now if you've forgotten about bends, we'll concentrate on air embolism. And that's hard to explain to somebody who doesn't know anything about diving. But I'll try. When a diver is down, the air he has in his lungs is at the same pressure as the water around him. Now the pressure of the water around keeps changing as the divers goes up and down. It changes half a pound per square inch for every foot the diver ascends or descends. Right?"

"Right," said the priest.

"Now if a diver goes down six feet and doesn't take a breath, the water pressure around him has increased three pounds per square inch, but the pressure in his lungs has remained the same, because he's holding his breath. There's three pounds per square inch less pressure in his lungs than in the water. But that doesn't bother him. The human body and lungs can take a tremendous amount of exterior pressure without hurt. That's why skin divers can go down a hundred feet just on the air they take in on the surface, where the pressure is much less.

"Now think of what happens if the diver holds his breath and comes up six feet. The pressure of the water around him goes down three pounds. Which means, putting it another way, that he has three pounds per square inch more pressure in his lungs than there is in the water around. His lungs expand like a balloon, the tissue rips, and if he's not real lucky, he dies. That's called air embolism and that's what that guy died of."

Father Bredder considered this for a moment. "An experienced diver would surely know about this danger, wouldn't he?" he asked.

"Yes," said Bob. "But there are still a lot of guys who manage to get hold of diving equipment and go diving without any proper instruction."

"This man—was it established whether he had had any experience?"

"They only just got identification on him," said Bob. "His name was Philip Northcote. . . ."

"Not Northcote—Norwood," said Bill.

"Okay," said Bob. "His name was Philip Norwood and, while he wasn't really experienced, he was certified. That means he'd gone through a proper course of instruction and passed his examination."

"So he would know about air embolism?"

"Sure."

"And his gear was in order and there was air in his tank?"

"Right."

"And holding his breath and ascending would kill him?"

"Deader than a mackerel," said Bill cheerfully.

"Sort of like suffocation," said Father Bredder.

"No. Not suffocation. Air embolism. He had air and he could have breathed in and out. But he didn't.

"That's what I mean by suffocation," said Father Bredder. "He had air, but he didn't or couldn't use it." He was thinking of Dr. Tighler.

Nine

BARBARA WENT to the dance that evening. She went with Rick, and Rick, his face scrubbed to the suggestion of a shine and his red hair the subject of half an hour's grooming, called for her. This had not been his original intention. He had proposed to meet Barbara at the dance, but Father Bredder had taken the opportunity of calling at the hot dog stand and having a word with Rick. Barbara had told him of this arrangement, and the priest had pointed out that this wasn't quite what should be done.

"You're going to the dance with Barbara tonight?" he asked.

"Yes," said Rick. "I'm going to meet her there. Saves time," he added by way of a tattered excuse.

"It won't do that way," said the priest. "You must call for her and speak to her father first."

"Cripes, but he's a cop," said Rick.

"Yes. And I'm a priest," said Father Bredder.

"Gee," said Rick in dismay, seeing here two tremendous handicaps to his evening.

"And someday you're going to be a man," Father Bredder went on. "Which means that you must accept the responsibilities of manhood, not the least of which is that of taking care of your date. So you must call at the house and see her father and get permission to take Barbara out. That doesn't scare you, does it?"

"No. It doesn't scare me. But it's kind of old-fashioned. Usually a bunch of guys just go to that dance and meet a bunch of girls there."

"Let me tell you something," said Father Bredder. "Girls are basically old-fashioned. Even when they seem to be otherwise. They appreciate being called for. And brought back home. Without worries and without having to be a little underhanded with their parents about their dates."

Rick considered this for a while. He'd dated girls before and called at their homes to pick them up. But on Catalina nobody was that formal. He didn't want the other guys to think he was going steady with Barbara. He just liked her, that was all.

"We're not going steady," he said. "We're just friends."

"I think you are both a little young to be going steady," said the priest. "But Barbara is still a girl and, as I said, girls are a little old-fashioned. The harder they pretend they are not, the more they appreciate these courtesies."

"Okay," said Rick. "I'll call for her. Say, if you're a priest, how do you know so much about girls?"

"I have about two hundred girls in my care," said Father Bredder. "If you need any advice, ask me. I'm an expert."

So Rick called for Barbara, and it amused Father

Bredder that Minardi was almost as embarrased as the young man. He tried to make some small talk but couldn't and offered Rick a cup of coffee and Rick said he didn't drink coffee. And then there was a strained silence while Father Bredder sat on the settee and chuckled quietly.

Barbara, of course, was not ready. The priest knew she wouldn't be ready, for she was exercising the ancient stratagem of keeping her date waiting so as not to appear too anxious to go out with him. When she appeared, she was wearing a lime-colored semi-formal which went beautifully with her slightly olive skin and dark hair, and her father stood up as she entered the room and stared at her as if seeing her for the first time. She wasn't a young girl in beach shorts and a halter any more. She was a young woman—and very lovely.

"We'll be back at eleven," said Rick, and fled with Barbara through the door.

"She's grown up," said Minardi. "It's hard to believe."

"It always is," said Father Bredder, who remembered baptizing Barbara not so many years ago. "It's sad and yet it's wonderful."

"She looked like her mother," said Minardi, and to this the priest said nothing.

"I suppose we ought to stay home tonight since Barbara's out," said Minardi.

"No. We ought not," said the priest firmly. "I'm not going to spend the evening with you playing cribbage while you keep looking at your watch."

"You're right," said Minardi. "There's a little Italian place down the end of the street here where they serve good Escallipino of Veal. And the beer's draft. Though we should drink wine with scaloppine."

"I like beer," said Father Bredder. "Cold. Wine doesn't go with a pipe and tobacco."

The restaurant was called Tipi's and was at the east end of the town, near the ocean front. It had the usual flagged floors and checkered tablecloths, and the lights were contained in chianti bottles hung from the ceiling. There was a small and dimly lit bar in one corner, open to the restaurant. They sat at a table in the far corner and ordered veal, with beer for Father Bredder and a red Napa Valley wine for Minardi. After a little while, when the priest had got his pipe going (his first pipe of the day, for he was trying to cut down on smoking), a man came in and sat at the bar which was near the entrance. Even in the subdued light Father Bredder recognized him."

"That man at the bar," he said. "He is following me, I think. He was on the beach when we were talking together and followed me to the pier while you took a nap. There he is now."

"That was to be expected," said Minardi moodily. "Though Redwood ought to use someone with a little more skill."

"Redwood?" asked the priest.

Minardi explained what had happened between him and his chief and, far from resenting Redwood's suspicions, Father Bredder was deeply interested in them.

"He's right," he said.

"What do you mean, he's right?" asked Minardi.

"That you are a connecting link between Tighler and Bodetkin, and that, having murdered Tighler, you went back to Bodetkin's room to destroy some evidence linking one to the other?"

"No. Not that," said the priest. "Because I didn't kill Tighler. And at the time I was in Bodetkin's room, I didn't even know that Tighler had been killed. But I sense a connection between the two, though I don't know what it is. Books mostly." He told Minardi of Tighler and Bodetkin having the same books. Minardi shrugged it off.

"There isn't any connection there at all," he said. "Absolutely none. Pure coincidence. I could go into a hundred houses in Los Angeles and find identical book titles. If only you hadn't gone back to Bodetkin's room after you left me, you wouldn't be in this ridiculous situation. You utterly deprived yourself of any alibi, and if Redwood can dig up anything that looks like a motive, you'll be on trial for murder in the first degree."

Father Bredder took a sip of his beer and nodded his head in appreciation of the flavor. "That's good beer," he said. "Tastes like Philippine beer. I had some in the war and I still remember it."

"We were talking about you and your lack of an alibi," said Minardi testily.

"Well, that's in our favor," said Father Bredder.

"I suppose it would also be in our favor—your favor —if Redwood dug up a motive connecting you with Tighler's murder?"

"Of course it would," said the priest. "That would really be excellent. Because I'm looking for much the same thing."

"Maybe I spent too much time out in the sun," said Minardi, "so my brain's not working. Explain, please."

"As to the alibi," said Father Bredder. "The really helpful part is that Tighler was murdered while I was searching Bodetkin's room."

"I don't see anything helpful in that," said Minardi.

"That's because you are not doing your job properly. You are trying to protect me, and that's not your job. Your job is to find out who murdered Tighler and nothing more. If I am the murderer, then your job is to devote your very best efforts to proving my guilt. I really do beg you to try your best to find the murderer and forget about any friendship between us." Father Bredder paused. "I would be very sad if our friendship interfered with your doing your work properly," he said.

"Let's get back to the alibi," said Minardi. "How does it help that you haven't one?"

"Because whoever was guilty of the murder knew that at the time of the crime I would be in Bodetkin's room unknown to anybody. Or if he didn't know I would be in Bodetkin's room, he knew at least that I would be somewhere without a witness to prove where I was. That suggests a close knowledge of my intended whereabouts on that night. And that's really surprising. Because when I left you, I had not intended to go anywhere but back to the convent—a bus journey at that time of the night of no more than twenty-five minutes from your apartment.

"I got off the bus at Seventh and Figuroa, walked down Seventh and was passing the Porter Hotel when I remembered that I still had the key to Bodetkin's room. On the spur of the moment I decided to use it once more to search the room before returning it. So we are up against a superlative mind reader."

"I can't buy that," said Minardi. "Nobody can read anybody's mind that closely."

"Perhaps not," said Father Bredder. "The point I am making is that the murderer timed his impersonation in such a way as to leave me without an alibi. He might have taken a chance. But it is much more likely that he planned it."

"Who has so close a knowledge of you that he could foresee that, passing the Porter Hotel, you would be struck by the thought that you ought to return the key and then struck by the further thought that you ought to take a last look around Bodetkin's room?" asked Minardi. The question was slightly sarcastic.

"I don't know," said Father Bredder. "I'll have to think about it. Only Father Armstrong knew I was going to be out that night. But he knew I was going to be with you, and there would be no better alibi than that. He couldn't possibly have known that on my way back I would stop at the hotel and be there for two hours. But whoever knew or guessed that I would go back to the Porter Hotel also knew that Tighler had called me, otherwise the impersonation wouldn't work."

"And do you know of anyone who was in possession of that piece of information?"

"Only Father Armstrong, to my present knowledge," said Father Bredder. "But he was at the convent all the time."

"How do you know he was at the convent?"

"Actually I don't know," said Father Bredder. "He said he was. I don't think he would have any difficulty in proving it. Anyway, he took your telephone message for me."

"How long have you known Father Armstrong?" asked Minardi.

"Two years."

"What was he before he became a priest?"

"He was one of the faculty of Oxford University in England."

"What did he teach?"

"English Literature."

The dinner had been brought and Minardi busied himself for a while with his veal.

"Everything seems to be floating in the air," he said at length. "Let's try to nail something to the floor. The one thing I would like to nail to the floor is the motive. If we can find a motive for the murder of Tighler, we can find a trail leading to the murderer. Murder—real murder—is a reasonable and logical act because it is done for a specific purpose. Find the purpose, and you find out who profits by the murder and therefore who is the killer. And in your case there isn't a shred of motive because there is no connection at all between you and Tighler. No connection at present and no connection in your background."

"You know all about my background?" asked Father Bredder jokingly.

"Yes," said Minardi. He wasn't joking. "I've looked you up right back to your boyhood. I did it when we first met. It is routine procedure with me to investigate the background of anyone with whom I become friendly. Because of my profession, I have to be sure that I am not being used."

Father Bredder's respect for his friend increased considerably with that admission. "You are right about the motive," he said. "It's important. Actually I have a suspicion concerning the motive. But I can't tell you about it because it would only confuse you. I haven't worked it out clearly myself because I haven't got all the facts. The main things that worry me are the petunias and why Bodetkin died of a heart attack."

"Oh, for goodness' sakes, will you never forget about Bodetkin?" asked Minardi.

"Bodetkin's death is linked to Tighler's murder," said the priest. "It is only the heart attack that worries me. That and the petunias."

At that moment the waiter came to the table and said that Minardi was wanted on the telephone. The detective had hardly left the table before the man with the square face and short cropped hair who had been sitting at the bar walked toward the rear of the restaurant where there was a second exit. He passed Father Bredder's table on his way and, as he did so, said loud enough for the priest to hear, "Psalm One twenty-nine. After midnight on the pier. And don't tell the copper."

Father Bredder didn't have to look up the Psalm. He knew it by heart. It went:

"Out of the depths I have cried unto thee, O Lord; Lord, hear my voice. . . ."

"Out of the depths," said Father Bredder to himself. "Out of the depths." It was a little while before he remembered the drowned scuba diver they had found while fishing off the Hermosa Beach Pier. He said nothing to Minardi, who returned to report that there was no one on the line when he answered the telephone.

Ten

LIEUTENANT MINARDI was a man who was careless of sleep. He could go for several days on four or five hours' sleep every night, and he believed that the body took as much rest in the form of sleep as it needed and anything beyond that was pure sloth. Quite frequently he was awake until three or four in the morning and yet reported for work punctually at nine, as fresh as others who had put eight hours unconscious in their beds. When he was tired, he could sleep anywhere, and so it was not a strange bed and surroundings to which he had not yet become accustomed that kept him awake in the bungalow in Avalon. Nor was it his daughter and her date, for Barbara had returned from the dance at eleven, talked about it in great excitement until midnight, and then been sent off to bed.

What kept him awake was the priest—the priest whose impersonator had killed Dr. Tighler by suffocation. The audacity of the impersonation bewildered him. If someone wanted to kill Dr. Tighler, why pose as Father Bredder in order to commit the crime? What hope had the murderer of sustaining that deception, of continuing to pin suspicion if not outright guilt on the priest when the priest could have no possible motive for the murder? There was no hope at all. Sooner or later the full facts would come out, the housekeeper would be proved mistaken, and the true identity of the murderer would be found. So it was an utterly senseless and childish deception unless its object had been nothing more than to gain admittance to Dr. Tighler.

That aspect was being checked by Redwood. He was working to find out whether somebody had called Tighler, identified himself as Father Bredder, and so arranged an appointment. A list of all telephone calls made from Tighler's home was being obtained, and the domestic staff were being questioned about all incoming telephone calls in the several days immediately preceding Tighler's death.

"That would be it, of course," Minardi assured himself. "The murderer knew that Tighler had contacted Father Bredder. How he knew, I don't know. But he must have known and he called Tighler, said he was Father Bredder, that he had thought the matter over, was prepared to help him, and arranged an appointment. Then, dressed as the priest, he gained admission and killed his victim. His only objective was murder, and he had no plan for pinning the guilt for long on Father Bredder, because a motive would be lacking."

The detective tried to convince himself of the truth of this conjecture, but didn't quite succeed. His mind was not easy with it, but for reasons he could not immediately identify. Something was wrong. He had not thought the matter through thoroughly. And the reason he had not done so was because he himself could not accept the thought of anybody really believing Father Bredder guilty of the cime.

He reached for a cigarette, pulled off the filter tip expertly and lit the cigarette. He inhaled the harsh smoke deeply, retained it in his lungs for a few seconds and slowly exhaled, having absorbed all the nicotine and tars possible into his system. He knew both were productive of cancer. But he had seen many people die many different deaths, and cancer did not particularly disturb him, whereas the raw tobacco smoke gave him pleasure and served to sharpen his wits.

"All right," he said, continuing his meditation. "Let us swallow the bull, horns and all, and accept the theory that the murderer impersonated Father Bredder both to gain admission to his victim and to pin the guilt of the murder on Father Bredder. That means that the murderer knew of something between Father Bredder and Tighler so reprehensible that Father Bredder could conceivably have killed Tighler to destroy the evidence of whatever it was. But the two never met. At least Father Bredder says they never met. And I've never known him to tell a lie before."

He thought over all he knew of the priest. He had been a Marine Corps Sergeant, serving in the Pacific Area during World War II. Immediately after his discharge, he had entered a seminary and become a priest. That was quite a change for a Sergeant of Marines. Father Bredder had explained to him once how it had come about. He had been using a flame thrower on a Japanese concrete gun emplacement. A Jap had run out screaming, wreathed in flames and running while he was burning to death. And Sergeant Bredder, as he was then, had been overcome with the horror of it all, and wondered whether that was indeed what he had been born for and raised on a small farm in Ohio—to burn his fellow men alive. And so he had become a priest.

Well, it was a good enough reason for a man to become a priest, he supposed. Stranger changes had taken place in individuals as a result of one climactic experience. But was that the true reason? Might it not be that Father Bredder, as a Sergeant of Marines, had been guilty of some terrible negligence or breach which had been covered up but for which he felt he had to atone by taking Holy Orders? Perhaps in some desperate situation he had turned coward and left his men to be exterminated, and only Tighler knew about it, and now Tingler had threatened to expose him.

It was possible. And Redwood was looking into that, too—Normal Redwood, with his Wednesday Rotary luncheon and his tenacious, unimaginative routine and enormously effective method of inquiry.

The odd aspect of this last supposition, positing a motive on Father Bredder's part for killing Tighler, was that Father Bredder was not in the least worried. He even welcomed inquiry into a motive and had warned Minardi himself not to let friendship interfere with his police duties.

Minardi jabbed his cigarette out in the ashtray and, walking to the front door, flung it open and went for a moment into the soft night air. The street was ashen with moonlight, the shadows of the date palms and oleanders around lying like lines and pools of dark liquid on the silvery road. He glanced down the street toward the bay. Someone was standing at the corner but moved out of sight. Minardi shrugged and returned to the living room.

He decided it was time to go to bed, and yet his mind would not leave the problem of the preposterous impersonation of Father Bredder and how the murderer had hoped to get away with it. And then, as he stood in his bedroom and was unbuttoning his shirt, he saw it. All that had to be done was to kill Father Bredder, but kill him in such a way that it would appear that he had committed suicide. There wouldn't then be any real need to hunt for a motive, for the suicide would be taken as a confession and a conviction. The housekeeper had seen Father Bredder visit Tighler. Tighler had been murdered. And then Father Bredder had killed himself. Even the police would regard the case as closed, and consider any hunt for a motive as being merely an exercise and a waste of time.

Minardi felt uneasy and glanced at his watch. It was half-past one. That was an odd time for someone to be hanging around at the corner of a street in Avalon. He rebuttoned his shirt and went to Father Bredder's room. There was a line of light coming from under the door, so the priest was not yet asleep. He knocked, got no answer, and pushed the door open.

The empty room, gaunt in the electric light, stared mockingly at him. Father Bredder was gone.

For a moment Minardi stood staring, shocked at the empty room. Even as he stared, that part of his mind which had been trained to this work was taking in the details and analyzing them. There was no suggestion of a struggle in the room. The bed had been sat on but not lain upon, evidenced by the disarray of the coverlet in the center. Father Bredder's pajamas were lying folded and ready for use on the pillow. There was a small table with a lamp by the bed, and on the table an ashtray. Some charred pipe tobacco lay in the bottom of the ashtray. The priest, on retiring, had smoked a pipe before getting ready to turn in.

Probably, the detective decided, he just went for a stroll. He would be back in a little while, and it was quite senseless to be disturbed by his absence. And yet the thought of the suicide plot made the detective uneasy. He decided, despite the hour, to look for the priest and went out by the back door, which would be the one the priest had used.

It led to a sand lot at the rear of the house, a lot which was fenced in with wire netting. An alleyway ran along the side of the house to the road in front and was the only exit from the fenced backyard. He followed this to the street and had started down the street toward the waterfront before he realized that he had no gun with him. His gun was still in his suitcase, and he considered for a moment going back for it. Then he decided not to.

What he was doing now would seem ridiculous in the morning. And yet he hurried down to the waterfront, which was the direction the priest was most likely to take, for the back end of the town was without appeal for a midnight stroll. When he reached the broad street fronting the bay, he looked to the left and right, but no one was in sight.

The moon was high in the sky, giving an astonishing whiteness to the sidewalks, the upper surfaces of the benches and the top of a low wall that flanked the beach. The pleasure pier, a highway of white satin, stretched out over the shimmering water, and further up to the left lay the steamer pier, in darkness from the buildings and palms that crowded around it.

A man was slouched on a bench at the foot of the pleasure pier, and Minardi crossed the street to question him. The man was asleep and when awakened was angry. He raised a belligerent face to the detective and Minardi recognized Shiny, the Main Street hanger-on whom he had seen, surprisingly, on the Hermosa Beach Pier while fishing with Father Bredder.

"Why don't you leave me alone, copper?" demanded Shiny. "You getting paid to follow me around?"

"Not specifically," said Minardi. "Who's paying you?"

"What d'yer mean, paying me? Ain't nobody paying me. I'm independent. Make my own living."

"Hanging around piers," said Minardi. "That's new territory for you, Shiny. Come on. What are you doing here?"

"Minding my own business, and why don't you mind yours?"

For answer Minardi reached down, grabbed Shiny by the shoulders and with seemingly very little effort jerked him to his feet.

"Listen, Shiny," he said. "I'm in a hurry. Have you seen Father Bredder down here tonight?"

"Who's Father Bredder?"

"You know who Father Bredder is. Have you seen him?"

"No. I ain't seen him." But in making the reply Shiny gave a surreptitious glance toward the head of the pier. Minardi thrust him back forcibly on the bench and ran down the pier. When he got to the end, he heard something that had been inaudible before—the soft puttering of a powerboat out in the bay. The water was so bright with moonlight that for a while he could not see the vessel. Then he caught a glimpse of a small beetle-like object which was passing out of the direct path of the moon.

He saw, rather than heard, a splash by its side and for a second concluded that the powerboat was a fishing vessel laying lobster pots. He sprinted down to the landing jetty where a small open cruiser lay with an outboard motor on the back. He fumbled for the choke, moved the throttle to the starting position, pulled the cord and the engine started immediately.

The splash couldn't have been a lobster pot. It was made by something heavy and bulky. Lobsters were out of season and, anyway, pots were illegal in Avalon Harbor. He headed the cruiser directly for the place where the splash had occurred, perhaps half a mile offshore.

The other boat immediately circled around and looked for a moment as if it were heading back toward him. Then it turned to sea again, and the engines were cut. A powerful searchlight was directed on the area where the splash had occurred. Then came the sound of a rifle being fired, but the little jet of flame from the barrel was directed downward.

A moment later a diver emerged from the water, climbed on the launch, and the launch took off in a surge of phosphorescence, headed for the mainland.

Minardi did not give chase, for to do so would have been foolish. He steered instead for the approximate location of the splash and saw something floating in the water, something that moved feebly as in the last stages of desperate struggle. He was alongside in a moment, cut the engine and, reaching over, pulled Father Bredder by the shoulders into the cruiser.

His arms were tied behind him and his feet were bound together. He was unconscious and, although there was a flicker of a heartbeat, he was not breathing. Minardi forced the priest's mouth open and started giving him mouth-to-mouth resuscitation. It was several minutes before the flickering heartbeat picked up and became steady and the priest started to breath of his own accord. He opened his eyes and looked at Minardi and said, quite solemnly, "Psalm One twenty-nine. 'Out of the depths have I cried unto thee, O Lord.'"

Then he fainted.

Eleven

"IF THERE IS one piece of advice that I would give to an innocent world," said Minardi, "it is this: If anyone tells you 'don't tell the cops,' go immediately to the police." He looked reprovingly at Father Bredder. "I'm surprised at you," he said. "You should have known better."

It was the afternoon of the following day. The priest had quite recovered from the attempt on his life and had refused any medical examination. He had also asked Minardi to make no mention of the attempt to anyone— the local police and especially to Barbara, though Minardi would have to report to Redwood. An ordeal which might have rudely shaken the nerves of other men had left Father Bredder unperturbed. Indeed, he was more distressed over the reproof of the detective than the incident that had brought on that reproof.

"I suspected that someone would try to kill me," said the priest. "It was the only solution possible to the impersonation of me by the murderer of Dr. Tighler. And yet, knowing that, I didn't suspect those two divers. I haven't got a very good mind. I mean it isn't agile enough. I didn't suspect an attempt at drowning me. Drowning is such an unusual method of murder. That's why I didn't think of it."

"When did you start suspecting that someone would try to kill you?" asked Minardi.

"After Dr. Tighler's housekeeper had identified me as the man who was with him shortly before he was suffocated."

"And why didn't you tell me?" demanded the detective. "I sat up half the night trying to figure that out, and I only got it just in time. If I hadn't been wrestling with the whole problem after Barbara went to bed, you would be dead as a mackerel right now."

"I relied on my guardian angel," said Father Bredder.

Minardi looked suspiciously at the priest. "Are you trying to tell me that your guardian angel told me to do some thinking on this subject and then suggested a possibility that saved your life?" he asked, pronouncing each word with deliberation.

"Well, of course that isn't the major task of guardian angels," said the priest. "They are more concerned with danger to the soul. But in their off hours, as it were, they guard against physical danger. How else do you explain arriving at the solution?"

"Pure deduction," said Minardi.

"That's a good name," said Father Bredder.

"A good name for whom?"

"A good name for your guardian angel," said the priest. "Pure Deduction. I call mine Joe. It's a liberty, but if I called him by some more formal title, we couldn't really be friends."

Minardi sighed. "Let's get back to something practical like your little midnight swim," he said. "Tell me how it all happened. Only this time, stick to the point and keep the angels out of it."

"All right," said the priest. "You are aware of a man who had been following me around. He came over on the steamer with me and was on the beach when you were with me the first day and followed me down to the pier while you had a nap. He was also in Tipi's when we had dinner. You thought he was from the police department, and so did I when you mentioned Captain Redwood's suspicions. He came to the table when you were away on that fake telephone message and said, 'Psalm One twenty-nine. After midnight on the pier. But don't tell the cop.' I knew then that he wasn't from the police department, and I guessed that he had some information to give me about the drowned diver."

"What drowned diver?" asked Minardi.

"Philip Norwood—the one we found when we were fishing off the pier in Hermosa Beach."

"Good Lord," said Minardi. "What's he got to do with Tighler?"

"Tighler and Bodetkin," said the priest. "I don't know yet, but I think it's all connected. I can't tell you why because it's a sort of spiritual connection that is hard to put into words. I have something, however, that you can hold on to.

"Philip Norwood, the drowned driver, wasn't drowned and I don't think his death was an accident. He died of a condition called air embolism which is a hazard attached to diving of which all trained drivers are well aware. It's wrong to call it suffocation, but its first essential is not breathing or being unable to breathe, which is the same as suffocation. Tighler died of suffocation, and the first step in the death of Norwood was, as it were, suffocation or not breathing. So there's a relationship. You will admit, won't you, that murderers usually have a favorite method?"

"Yes," said Minardi.

"Well, our murderer's favorite method is suffocation. Put your doubts aside and accept Norwood and Tighler as victims of the same man. Both died basically of inability to breathe. And that was the death chosen for me."

"Who told you all this about Norwood?" asked Minardi.

"The Meistrell twins," said Father Bredder, and explained about his interview with them.

"All right, back to yourself," said Minardi. "You kept an appointment with this man because you suspected that he could tell you something about the death of Norwood. What happened then?"

"When I got to the pier shortly after midnight," said the priest, "it was deserted except for someone sleeping on the bench at the entrance."

"Shiny," said Minardi.

"Was that really Shiny?" asked Father Bredder. "That's interesting."

"Yes. Shiny is about to be investigated pretty thoroughly. Go on."

"I walked down the pier to the landing stage where the pleasure boats tie up and saw two divers on board a power cruiser. They were dressed in their diving gear. I thought they were the Meistrell twins and it was only when I got on board at their invitation that I discovered they were strangers."

"Did they say anything?"

"Yes. One of them, a man of about my size, said, 'There's something on the bottom of the ocean that we want you to see.' The other said, 'It isn't the kind of thing that can be done in daylight.' He had a rather high-pitched voice."

"And what did you say?"

"I said 'just what kind of a thing is it?' And the big one replied. 'You'll know soon enough.' "

"And that was all that was said?"

"Yes. I was aboard by that time. They cast off in a second and headed out of the bay. The steering wheel was at one side of the cockpit behind a windscreen and I stood at the other side. I felt uneasy but didn't know why. I soon knew, however, when I felt something in my back and was told by the man who was not steering that he had a gun on me, that I was to put my hands behind me and not cry out or I would be shot."

"Did you cry out?" asked Minardi.

"No. I would have, had there been any sense to it. But the engine noise would have overwhelmed any shout I could give, and the only source of help was the sleeping man—Shiny—on the pier already several hundred yards behind. Of course by this time I knew that they were going to drown me and what I would see at the bottom of the ocean would be death."

"Try to remember everything they said," said Minardi.

"They had some discussion about putting a weight belt on me. One, the smaller, said that if they put a twenty-pound weight belt on me and pushed me over the side, I'd go straight down and be dead in a few minutes. Then they could both dive down, find me, take off the weight belt, untie my hands and feet and I would float to the surface and it would look like just plain drowning—suicide.

"The other, the bigger one, told him not to be a fool. He said that the pressure deep down would break my eardrums and various blood vessels and any doctor would be able to tell that I'd been murdered. I had to be drowned in a few feet of water, so that the effects of pressure wouldn't show and all would appear more natural. It was just a matter of holding my head under long enough, just below the surface, so I was forced to open my mouth and breathe in the water."

"You struggled, of course," said Minardi.

"Not to much effect," said Father Bredder. "They had it all well thought out. When they were sufficiently far offshore, the engine was cut and, between the two of them, they tied my hands and feet. Then they made me lie face down on the cockpit and they wrapped a large length of cloth around me as if I were a mummy. That was clever because even though the cloth wasn't tied on, it prevented me using legs and arms which were tied, anyway. It kept them together. Then it was just a matter of starting the engine again, taking me further out and dumping me overboard.

"One of the divers went right after me, grabbed me by the shoulders and pushed my head down. And I'm afraid I would have been killed except for Joe."

"Joe?"

"My guardian angel. You see, when I was talking to the Meistrell twins about Norwood, I asked them a lot of questions about diving, and the subject of drowning naturally came up. They told me that most drownings were really death by shock—that is, a massive shock to the system as a result of taking water into the lungs. There is rarely enough water in a drowning victim's lungs to have caused death by displacement of the air. It's shock. So they said that if in a dangerous situation you could just control the increasing insistence of the lungs on breathing, you had a much better chance of survival.

"I asked them how that could be done, because in the Marines I used to try holding my breath in a tight situation where a single sound or movement would give me away, and there came a point where I had to breathe even if it killed me.

"They said all that you had to do was to swallow. If you swallow, the desire to take a breath is instantly relieved. Skin divers do this frequently. Skin divers, you know, are divers who go down without aqualungs or any artificial air supply. But there's a danger, because if you keep on swallowing, you become unconscious because the oxygen supply in the air in the lungs falls below what can support life. Nonetheless, the swallowing technique can permit you to hold your breath for a surprisingly long time."

"So you swallowed and when they put your head under, you were able to hold on for a time?"

"Yes. But I was helped by the cloth they had wrapped around me. You see it came loose in the water and tangled the diver who was trying to drown me. And he had to keep wrestling with it as well as with me. And whenever he did, I had a chance to get a little breath, though I got a little water, too."

"How long did this go on?" asked Minardi.

"Five Our Fathers," said the priest.

"You were praying?"

"Certainly. It was the only sensible thing to do. Eventually they took the cloth off me altogether, and the diver got hold of my feet and started to swim down with them, ignoring the depth he took me to. There was a terrible wedging sensation in my ears and a sharp pain, but surprisingly it went whenever I swallowed, which I had to do more and more frequently. But gradually I started to suffocate. It wasn't unpleasant. My head got swimmy and I couldn't concentrate. Bits and pieces of thoughts or impressions came into my mind, all unconnected with one another. I had my eyes shut because when I was a boy I was once frightened opening them underwater. But I opened them and saw only lovely silver globes streaming upward in utter blackness. Then I lost consciousness and you know the rest. But it taught me something well worth knowing."

"What?" asked Minardi.

"I think I was fairly close to death, and what I learned is that death isn't terrible. Nothing to be frightened of at all. Of course, I should have known that before."

"Why should you have known that before?"

"Because God loves us," said Father Bredder. "He wouldn't frighten his children at the end."

To that Minardi made no immediate comment. "Would you recognize either of these two men again?" he asked.

"I might be able to," said Father Bredder. "I might recognize their voices and their general build. One, I am sure, was the man who gave me the message in the restaurant. I would recognize him, I believe. But you must remember that they were in those rubber diving suits and had on hoods, which exposed the face only from the lower lip to above the eyebrows. And although it was bright moonlight, that isn't the best light for seeing people's faces by. I would recognize the other more readily if I saw him in a diving suit again."

"The odd thing is that with all the struggling you must have done, you didn't collect any bruises."

"No. That's not odd at all," said Father Bredder. "You see they had soft rubber mittens on their hands. They could grip me without bruising me."

"And they used strips of the same rubber to tie your hands and feet, with the same idea," said Minardi. "You were to be found drowned and with no visible marks so it would be taken as suicide. Did you notice anything about their diving gear that was unusual?"

"I'm not very familiar with diving gear," said the priest. "So if there was anything unusual, I wouldn't know. But I thought we could talk to the Meistrell twins about that. In fact I've already arranged an occasion for doing so."

"What occasion?" asked Minardi.

"Well, they took a liking to me and asked whether I would like to go albacore fishing tomorrow in their boat. That was before this happened, so I accepted for both of us."

"You're a strange man, Father Bredder," said Minardi, shaking his head. "I should think after your experience, the last thing you would want to do would be go out on a boat with a couple of divers."

"Oh, we mustn't miss it," said the priest. "The alba-core are really beginning to run, and I've never caught an albacore in my life. And I want to learn to dive, and I think that while fishing I can persuade the Meistrells to agree to teach me."

"What ever do you want to learn to dive for?" asked the detective.

"Psalm One twenty-nine—'Out of the depths . . .' " replied Father Bredder.

Twelve

THEY MET the Meistrell brothers, Bob and Bill, at the
pier at one that afternoon. They had a live bait tank on
board their boat and three poles.

"You got the wrong kind of hooks," said Bill. "Those
are halibut hooks."

"Well, that's what you use to get albacore. The boy at
the store said everybody's using them," said Bob.

"That's because he wasn't selling any halibut hooks.
Albacore hooks have a reverse barb—the tip's bent back
a bit."

"Listen. What do you use for bait for albacore?"

"Live anchovy."

"Okay. And what do you use for bait for halibut?"

"Anchovy."

"Just what I said. The hook goes into the anchovy
first. So it's the same hook."

"You trying to tell me that there's no difference between a halibut and an albacore?"

"No. I'm just telling you that there's no difference between one anchovy and another. Let's go."

Bill took the wheel, and Bob started tying hooks on
the lines. Every now and then he would tell Bill not to go

112 ·

so fast or quit swerving the boat around, and Bill would tell him to mind his business and get the lines ready. They rounded the east end of Catalina and saw, out in the Pacific and north of San Clemente, a congregation of boats, perhaps twenty of them, spread around in an area of two square miles, marking the place where the albacore were running.

The ocean, even on the windward side of the island, was smooth and blue, seemingly the more peaceful because of a gentle swell rolling lazily in from the north.

"Do you ever get albacore with a spear gun?" Father Bredder asked Bob, to bring up the subject of diving.

"No. They're too fast. You can get yellowtail and white sea bass and grouper, and so on. They swim fairly slowly. But albacore are like jet bombers. You'll see. When they take off, give them plenty of line."

"Give him the Star drag," said Bill. "That's the best reel."

"Will you quit telling me what to do?" retorted Bob. Then he gave Father Bredder the Star drag. Minardi got a rod with an Italian reel on it. They fished for three hours and caught twenty-three albacore between them before they ran out of live bait. They they let the *Linda Kay* drift on the gentle ocean swell while they cleaned up and ate some sandwiches and drank Cokes.

Catching the fish had been both exciting and strenuous. Father Bredder was astonished at the swiftness and strength of the albacore, with their long pectoral fins, which they spread like the swept-back wings of an airplane. They had great power and speed and boating one, even for so powerful a man as he, often took twenty minutes of tremendously hard work.

He lost several hooks before, under Bob's instruction, he learned to let the hooked fish have plenty of line to run with when it had taken the bait. His hands and arms and back ached from reeling his catches in, but he was pleased to see a faint glow of pink on Minardi's cheeks and have him, even for a little while, lose his aspect of concern.

Munching the sandwiches, Bob was telling Bill that they ought to have brought more live bait, and Bill was saying that if they brought more they would have died in the tank through overcrowding, to which Bob replied that if they had fitted a bigger pump, as he said they should have, that wouldn't be a problem. The exchanges between the twins were always sharp, but they were never vicious, for they had a profound attachment to each other. Father Bredder reflected how fortunate the two were, for the quarrels which other men had with themselves, the brothers had with each other.

"Tell me something more about diving," said the priest, interrupting a minor skirmish on whether more albacore would have been caught if the "halibut" hooks hadn't been used. "Where do you get the oxygen?"

Bob and Bill exchanged looks of deep compassion with each other. "It's not oxygen," said Bill. "People get an idea that any gas that is put in a tank to breathe is oxygen. It's just air—compressed air. And you get your tank refilled at a dive shop for a dollar twenty-five a throw."

"There's a place where that can be done here on Avalon?" Minardi asked.

"Sure. Right on the end of the pier. But it costs a little more here than on the mainland."

"Is a record kept of who gets tanks filled?"

"No. Responsible dive shops, if they don't know the diver, ask to see his certificate that shows he's taken a course in diving. But that isn't always done. In fact, it isn't possible. Sometimes a diver asks a friend to get his tanks filled for him, and the friend may not be a diver at all."

"About the air station here," said Minardi. "Would the people who operate it know most of the divers for whom they filled tanks?"

"I don't know," said Bob. "They might. But there is an increasing number of new divers around every year. Why?"

"If you can keep a secret, I'll tell you," said Minardi.

"You don't have to tell me if you don't want to," said Bill.

Minardi looked at him speculatively. "It might help me to tell you. I'll take a risk that you can keep a secret. Two divers tried to drown Father Bredder the other night."

"You're kidding," exclaimed the twins in unison.

"No," said the detective, and told them the details.

"If we can find out who made the attempt, we can solve a lot of things," said Minardi. "Any suggestions that might lead to identifying these two thugs?"

"Did you notice anything particular about their gear?" asked Bob. "Here. I'll show you a diver's gear." He pulled open the top of one of the seats in the cockpit and started to fling out various pieces of equipment. He held up a weight belt. "Did the weight belt of the guy who

· *115*

tried to drown you look like that?" he asked. Father Bredder inspected it. The belt itself was of orange-dyed dacron and the weights were oblongs with the corners rounded off.

"No," he said. "It was different. It looked like an ammunition belt with the weights in pockets. Does that mean anything?"

"Yes. Those ammo belts are dangerous because there is no quick release fastener on them. Some of the old-time divers used them until they got smart. Some of them are so woodenheaded they still do. What about his regulator? Did it look like this?" He held up a twin hose regulator, the hoses made of rubber with a concertina fold.

"I can't be sure," said the priest. "But I think the hoses were shorter."

"Old style," said Bill. "What about his tank—was it galvanized like that?"

"No. It was painted. It seemed bigger. Fatter perhaps. But that may have been the moonlight."

"And his knife, did you see that?"

"No. It was in a scabbard."

"On his leg?"

"No. On his belt. Like a bayonet scabbard."

"Well," said Bob. "All his equipment was old and the weight belt and knife were improvised. I'd say he was someone who didn't go into dive shops much except to get his tank filled. Tell me more about the tank. Was it rounded on the bottom, or did it have a kind of a hollow in it at the bottom?"

"I can't say," said the priest. "But it looked a lot different from that tank."

"It wasn't a proper dive tank, then," said Bob. "It was converted from an industrial tank, maybe from a CO_2 fire extinquisher. You're not kidding about all this?"

"No," said Father Bredder. "I'm not."

"This diver would have had to have his tank filled with air at some time or another," said Minardi. "If his tank was special—converted into what you call a dive tank—then whoever filled it might remember it."

"Probably would," said Bill. "But the guy may have a compressor of his own and fill it himself."

"Does the description I gave you of the gear suggest any particular type of diver to you?" asked Father Bredder. "Does it suggest, for instance, someone who hadn't got enough money to buy proper equipment?"

"No," said Bob. "That's not likely to be it. It suggests a smart aleck—a guy who figures he knows it all and can design or improvise his own diving equipment. There're a few people like that in this diving business. They aren't really divers like the rest of the guys. That is, they don't dive for diving, but they dive to show that they're smarter than anybody else. I haven't got any time for them."

"Basically ignorant people?" asked Minardi.

"Uh-uh," said Bill. "You'd be surprised. Some of them are schoolteachers. Some of them are doctors. Some of them are engineers working, say, in an aircraft factory or a space laboratory. They all ought to know better. But they've got this thing about believing that they're smarter than the other dumb clucks, so they don't have to buy their gear like everybody else does. They can make it themselves. Some have all kinds of money. But buying gear, they figure, is for idiots. They'll take a fire extinguisher and turn it into a dive tank to show how smart they are. That tank you are talking about sounds like one of those."

"Would there be difficulty about getting such a tank filled with air?" asked Minardi. "I know I've asked that question before, but specifically, are tanks supposed to be pressure-tested before they can be legally filled?"

"You bet," said Bob. "They have an ICC number stamped on them to show the safe pressure to which they can be filled, and also a date. If the date is more than five years old, then the tank has to be pressure-tested again before it can be legally filled. Of course, there're always some places that will fill them. But no halfway decent dive shop will. In fact, it's dangerous. If one of those tanks exploded, it can knock down half a building."

"That gives us something to go on," said Minardi. "And in a way it fits—that is, if your guess that Father Bredder's friend was likely to be a man of some education. We have to find the owner of an odd-ball tank, using old or improvised diving gear, six feet tall, heavily built, and perhaps a professional man. How about the dive suit? Would he have to be measured for it somewhere?"

"Most are," said Bob. "We make hundreds of custom-tailored suits a year. But the kind of guy you're talking about is more likely to have made his own suit—either that or bought one from a mail-order house. There are a lot of places that supply ready-made suits in different stock sizes. They're cheaper than custom-made."

"And colder," said Bill. "They don't fit good. A lot of water gets in and out, and you get cold faster."

"This is the first lead we've had that has got any solidity to it," said Minardi. "The rest of the leads don't make any sense at all. I don't say that we have started getting somewhere. I can only say that we have stopped getting nowhere."

"There are some elements that fit into a pattern of a kind," said Father Bredder. "At least they do for me, but perhaps you wouldn't agree."

"What kind of elements?" said Minardi.

"The element of abuse," said Father Bredder. "The use of something but not for the purpose for which it was created. Books used for not-reading. Music used for not-listening to music. And diving used for murder instead of catching fish."

"Just a minute," said Minardi. "Apart from the attempt on you, I am quite sure that those two don't spend all their time diving to commit murder. They probably catch fish as well, like any other diver."

"I don't think so," said Father Bredder. "Only as a cover. They dive for some other purpose not normal to divers." He turned to the twins, who had been mystified by this exchange. "About Philip Norwood" he asked. "The body was found off the end of the Hermosa Beach Pier. Do you think that was the place he was drowned?"

"No. Couldn't be," said Bob. "He'd been in the water some time; three weeks, I think they estimated. He would have drifted in the currents from where he was when he died."

"Which way?" asked the priest.

"West," said Bob. "People think of it as north, but it's actually west."

"Will you quit confusing people," said Bill. "How can anybody goof up over north and west."

"Here's the thing," said Bob, ignoring his brother. "People think of California as running north and south and the Pacific Ocean lying to the west. But actually that part of the coast runs west, and Catalina Island, lying out in the Pacific, isn't actually west of Hermosa Beach; it's south. That's what I'm getting at. It doesn't matter except to get the directions right. Norwood, after he drowned, would have drifted loosely westward—not out into the ocean, but along the coast from a place east of Hermosa Beach which people would think of as being south of Hermosa Beach."

"There's a westerly inshore current?"

"Yes. Out in the channel the current runs east and south. Close to the coast it runs west, heading north eventually when the coastline permits. It's a countercurrent. It isn't fast. No more than half a knot. But it's there."

"From how far would that current take a body in three weeks?" asked Father Bredder.

The twins looked at each other. It was such a look as a man might give to a mirror when he wants to see his own reflection and be reassured by it.

"From Rocky Point," said Bob. "By Flat Rock."

"That's right," said Bill. "Rocky Point. That Jap kid that was fishing there turned up three weeks later on Hermosa Beach. Same time of the year, but a couple of years back."

"Is there anything at Rocky Point of special interest to divers?" asked Father Bredder.

"Sure. You can get lobsters there in season. Though not so many now. Sometimes yellowtail. There used to be abalone but they've been overfished now. What are left are undersized. There's a big fine for taking them out of season and undersized."

"Anything else—not connecting with sport?" asked the priest.

"Further down there's what's left of the *Dominator*. She's a Greek-owned Liberty ship that went up on the rocks in a fog several years ago. Some of it is on the bottom and some of it is on the reef."

"Then there's the barge," said Bill. "She tried to salvage the *Dominator* but got caught in heavy weather and foundered. She's on the bottom. Still leaking oil."

"Is that near Rocky Point?"

"No. Maybe a couple of miles further south," said Bill.

"East you mean," said Bob.

"Would it be possible for the drowned diver, Philip Norwood, to have been drowned near the barge and still have turned up in three weeks at the Hermosa Pier?"

"I guess so," said Bob. "But with a weight belt on he'd have rolled along the bottom and got caught on things which would have slowed him. They all come up if they're found at all on Hermosa Beach on Manhattan Beach. Because of the current and the way the coast heads out westward. If he drowned at Palos Verdes Point where the *Dominator* and the barge went down, he would take longer than three weeks, I'd say. But then you have to remember that it's only a guess that he was in the water three weeks. He could have been in longer. It's possible."

"I'd like to dive on that barge," said the priest. "Would you teach me to dive and then take me down on it?"

"The barge is in seventy-five feet of water," said Bob. "That's pretty deep for a novice diver. If there's anything you want to find down there, we could go down and look for it for you."

"There is something, I believe. But I'd have to look myself. I couldn't tell you what it is. I don't really know myself. I would know when I found it."

"Okay," said Bob. "We'll teach you. But we won't give you a certificate until you complete the full course. And you've got to promise never to dive alone. That's how Norwood was killed."

The priest filled his pipe from the crumpled envelope of tobacco he carried with him and said, "Norwood may have dived alone. But he wasn't alone when he died. He was murdered. Perhaps by a diver wearing an ammunition belt for his weights and a homemade dive tank."

Thirteen

WHEN MINARDI returned from his vacation, Normal Redwood had the results of his own investigation waiting for him. Those results consisted of thirty foolscap pages of names and addresses of people who had had any contact with Tighler and with Bodetkin. There were two lists—one for Tighler and one for Bodetkin. This was the Redwood bulldozer at work and performing at its highest efficiency. Redwood's method was to scoop up everything into a huge pile and then have Minardi sift through it—with a teaspoon.

The lieutenant both admired the job Redwood had done and was irritated by it. He admired the painstaking work that had gone into the compiling of these lists. The addresses were almost all included. Getting one address would often take a man half a day. But Redwood had them, having, of course, the assistance of his whole department. But he was irritated because of the huge pile of dross that was collected together with valuable information hidden in it and perhaps lost in it unless he took the pile apart, teaspoon by teaspoon, and examined each one as he scooped it out.

Attached to the list of addresses were fingerprints,

photographs—some from Tighler's house and some from Bodetkin's room. The fingerprints were part of the bulldozer work, too. Every single fingerprint had been taken and checked against the police files and then checked against the fingerprints of the domestic staff at Tighler's residence and the people at the Porter Hotel.

Most were the fingerprints that could be expected—those of chambermaids and other servants and mixed in with them those of Tighler in the case of his residence and Bodetkin in the case of the Porter Hotel. None of the fingerprints was recorded on police or FBI records. They were, then, the fingerprints of innocents, at least as far as the law had any record.

When he was handed these lists and photographs by Redwood, with instructions to investigate all persons on the list, question them, and ask them all they knew of Tighler's movements, his visitors, his telephone calls, his letters and anything else he could think of, Minardi allowed some of his irritation to show.

"Bodetkin, too?" he asked sarcastically. "You are aware that he died of a heart attack. You suspected Father Bredder and found in him a link between Tighler and Bodetkin. But surely you realize that the attempt to murder Father Bredder shows him innocent in Tighler's case and so destroys your link."

"If you want to be taken off the case, I can assign someone else to it," said Redwood.

"I don't want to be taken off the case," said Minardi. "I just want to spend my time profitably. The only murder we have is Tighler. I want your agreement that I should concentrate on Tighler. That's all."

"We have a murder and an attempted murder," said Redwood. "Concentrate on Tighler if that seems best to you. But keep Bodetkin in the back of your mind. Whoever tried to kill Father Bredder may have done so to carry off the impersonation. But he may have done so because he feared Father Bredder had found out something about Bodetkin or was likely to find out something about Bodetkin."

"For Heaven's sakes—a janitor?" demanded Minardi. "A janitor whom Simms, our own pathologist, says died of a perfectly normal heart attack?"

"A janitor who died of a heart attack and who had some peculiar hobbies for a man in his position and was able to spend some four thousand dollars on photographic equipment in six months out of a salary of eighty dollars a week. The coated lens and mounting in his enlarging camera cost close to a thousand dollars and was paid for in cash. Get that. Cash! Not bought by installments. Not paid for by check. But paid for in cash. Bodetkin didn't have a checking account that we can find. That's something else. Somebody was paying him to do something. He inconveniently died of a heart attack right in the middle of it. Then Tighler was murdered—by suffocation, which is damned peculiar, too." Redwood swung away from the desk to look out of the window at the top of the palm tree, caught in a glow of sunshine and smog, and he hated the artificiality of it as he always did.

"Damned peculiar," he said. "Not normal at all." Despite his irritation, Minardi smiled.

Redwood swung back to face the desk and eyed Minardi thoughtfully. A good detective, one of the best. But a Sicilian. A Latin. Sometimes they went into a kind of repose—a kind of stubborn disengagement which had an emotional base and out of which they had to be brought by hurting their pride. Then they got angry and worked.

"You're slipping on this case, Minardi," Redwood said deliberately. "You've achieved nothing, apart from letting Father Bredder get nearly murdered—and letting the murderer get away. You're not a professional any more."

It was the last sentence that told—that had the effect Redwood was looking for. Minardi's olive face turned lighter, giving his features an ashen look. His eyes were dark, glassy with anger. Redwood hit out again, deliberately. "You should have found out about that photographic equipment—not me," he said. "You should have compiled those lists. Not me. You went into this thing unconvinced of its importance and you're letting the department down."

"Is that all?" said Minardi, through lips as thin as cracked glass.

"That's all," said Redwood.

The detective got up, so angry he was shaking. He picked up the lists and for a moment looked as though he was going to hurl them at his chief. Then he strode to the door and opened it. As he went out, Redwood said, "Get Father Bredder in to see me."

The door slammed so hard that Redwood was not sure that Minardi had heard him. He picked up the telephone and told the operator, "Call Minardi and tell him I want him to get Father Bredder to see me at once. No. I don't want to talk to Minardi personally." He put the phone down and smiled. That was the last needed goad. Minardi would really be mad now. With some people you had to work that way—Latins mostly. And the Irish. People who were emotionally activated and weren't, then, normal and sensible in a Saxon kind of way.

Redwood had met Father Bredder before in connection with another case. He neither liked him nor disliked him, but he was puzzled by him. He found it hard to get concrete reliable facts out of the priest, because whatever process of deduction the priest used, it wasn't based on logic. At least it wasn't based on a logic that was recognizable as such. It was based on some kind of other dimension to which the words "mystical" or "spiritual" vaguely applied without in any degree describing it.

Captain Redwood's connection with the spiritual world was ordered and logical. He went to church every Sunday and passed the plate at the eleven o'clock service. It was the proper thing to do and he did it. He liked sermons with a practical text bearing on the duty of citizens to obey the law. He thought most of the epistles of St. Paul a lot of rubbish, though he was a sound man when it came to describing the proper relationship between a husband and wife. A wife should obey her husband, and a husband shouldn't go off chasing secretaries. That made sense, but much of the rest of the epistles didn't. Captain Redwood didn't look for sense in them. He concluded they had either been mistranslated or they were rubbish to start with. He had dealt with Minardi by making him angry. He would deal with Father Bredder by getting some plain facts out of him.

He succeeded nicely in getting the details of the attempted murder of the priest, but the going got boggy when the topic turned to Bodetkin. "I want the whole truth from you, Father," said Redwood. "Just why did you go back to Bodetkin's room that night?"

"I didn't intend to. But I had the key and Bodetkin worried me."

"Why did he worry you?"

"He had all those books, but no Bible," said the priest.

Redwood swallowed hard. "What's wrong with that?"

"It meant that he didn't really use the books for reading—he wasn't really a booklover."

"He might have been an atheist."

"The one book an atheist is sure to have is a Bible," said Father Bredder. "Otherwise he has nothing to misinterpret."

A few more questions got Redwood nowhere, and he turned to Tighler.

"You say you never met him, but he telephoned you. You were alone in his study when Minardi was talking to the housekeeper. Did you notice anything peculiar that struck you?"

"The books again."

"What about the books?"

"They had none of them been read through. They were the wrong books for such a man. But the housekeeper said he was often up late—reading. And reading not the scientific books but the other ones. Well, not reading them, but working with them."

"What do you mean by 'working with them'?"

"Getting something out of them, I think, that had nothing to do with their literary quality."

"Something like what?"

"I don't know. But I think it's connected with music."

"Oh, hell," said Redwood, forgetful of the priest. "How can you connect up books and music and a murder?"

"I don't know," said Father Bredder. "But you are right when you mention hell. That is, if hell is confusion, as I believe it to be—Milton's Pandemonium. And heaven is simplicity—intricate, exquisite simplicity."

Redwood shook his head vigorously, as a man submerged shakes his head on surfacing to get rid of the water. "You're not making sense," he said. "Let's get back to something normal. The books. You suspect something about the books Bodetkin had and the books Tighler had. We have found twenty titles they both possessed. You say they were not bought to be read. Take those twenty titles. If the two dead men having them in their possession isn't a coincidence, then what do you make of it?"

"Books can be used as a cipher," said Father Bredder. "People can pass secret messages around by reference to particular pages and lines in books. I think that might be investigated."

"And the music?"

"The odd thing about the music is that Bodetkin had lots of music—sheet music and records. But Tighler had none. Bodetkin had photographs of a music manuscript with two unrelated keys on the same photograph."

"Meaning what to you?"

"I think the music had a meaning other than music. I think it might have been a code that Bodetkin was devising or had devised."

"But not for Tighler, since Tighler didn't have any interest in music."

"Perhaps not for Tighler. I don't know. For somebody that he passed information on to."

"What kind of information?"

"I don't know. I can only guess that it was information that he received from Tighler and had to pass on to somebody else."

Redwood considered this for a while, and with growing suspicion. It sounded like a lot of nonsense, the sort of stuff that ran through the Sunday comics. Minardi might be right, after all. The only solid murder they had was the murder of Tighler by someone who had impersonated Father Bredder and later tried to kill Father Bredder.

"I'm looking for facts," he said. "This is all speculation. I don't like speculation. I like facts that lead from one to another and make a whole."

The reply the priest made surprised him. "Facts are a delusion," he said. "They are a delusion of truth as a mirage is a delusion of sight. The real facts lie in people's minds and not in fingerprints and books and photographs and all the other physical things which are only the accidents that occur as a result of what lies in the mind. Truth is a matter of the mind and all else is only a blurred shadow of that. Sometimes we have to use the blurred shadow to reconstruct the original image. But it is the image we are searching for."

Redwood sorted that out as best he could and said, "You mean motive."

"Motive, yes. But the frame of mind and the color of mind that permits the motive to grow and take effect."

Redwood grunted. "Both the men we are talking about are dead," he said. "That makes it difficult to get into their minds."

"The mind is part of the spirit and is never destroyed," said Father Bredder. "The effects of its workings linger on. The mind leaves fingerprints, and in the case of Tighler and Bodetkin there are plenty of fingerprints in the books and the music, and so on. It is those we have to work on. The artifacts themselves will tell us nothing. It is the spiritual fingerprints left on the artifacts that will give us our answers."

"Motive," said Redwood, clinging to the word as a man in deep water would cling to a log. Father Bredder smiled. Motive would have to be sufficient for Redwood for the time being, though he might grow a little later. He was like a man who, viewing a picture of a landscape, could see only the road going through it and none of the valleys, rivers, and woods around.

"May I ask you a question?" asked the priest.

"Certainly."

"Where was Bodetkin's car when he was found dead of the heart attack?"

"Highway 101, which, as you know, is also called Pacific Coast Highway. In Westchester, about a mile from his work. The car was pulled over to the side. The engine was switched off. He had managed to do that before he died."

"What was the nearest cross street?"

Redwood picked up a green folder off his desk, ruffled through the pages and said, "Manchester Boulevard."

"And at what time was he found?"

"Eight-thirty in the morning."

"He was only a mile from his work at the time?"

"Yes. About a mile."

"What time was he due at work?"

"Nine."

"So he would have been early," said the priest. "Who found him?"

"Mr. Peter Fells. He was on his way to San Diego and pulled over because he wanted some breakfast and saw a restaurant nearby. It's called The Huddle. He passed Bodetkin's car at the curb, glanced at him, saw he was either ill or dead, and called the police. Why?"

"It's a matter of a spiritual fingerprint," said Father Bredder. "They do not match."

"What do you mean?"

"A man dying of a heart attack might be able to pull his car to the side of the road," said the priest. "But I don't think he would interrupt his dying to turn off the engine."

Fourteen

IT TOOK Minardi an hour to get control of his anger and
start working effectively. During that time he raged in-
wardly at Redwood's stricture about not having made up
a list of names of people connected with Tighler. The
criticism was unjust, for there hadn't been time. Two
days after Tighler's death, he had been sent on vacation.
It was the injustice that rankled him, as Redwood knew it
would, and when he got himself under control, a cold
and vengeful anger remained with Minardi and he set to
work—to work with such intensity and energy that Redwood would have to apologize. This was just what Redwood wanted.

He looked over the list of Tighler's acquaintances,
picked up the telephone, made an appointment and then
sped out along the Harbor Freeway to see Dr. Edward
Simmons, of Intersystems. Dr. Simmons' secretary had
tried to stall about the appointment, but Minardi wasn't
in a mood for stalling. She said he had a meeting which
would keep him occupied all that afternoon, and could
he call tomorrow? And Minardi said, "This is a security
matter. The meeting can wait. I will be there at three
o'clock."

Dr. Simmons kept him waiting for ten minutes—just long enough to salvage his own pride, Minardi speculated. Then he was shown from the waiting room that looked like a showroom for Danish furniture into an office that looked like a movie director's impression of penthouse living in the twenty-first century.

The room was circular. The western semicircle of the wall was one enormous curtainless window. The sun, headed west, shone straight through the window but without a glare. Polarized, Minardi guessed. The room had a dome ceiling, and on the ceiling, to his surprise, shone the stars of the heavens, as in the dome of a planetarium. In the center of the room was a complicated instrument shaped like a dumbbell—a planetarium projector. There were chairs around, Swedish-type chairs with unstained wood arms and legs. Buttons on the arms of the chairs indicated that they could be tilted backward. Dr. Simmons' office, then, if this was his office, was a small planetarium, and Minardi decided that this was the new kind of scientist—a showman-scientist selling science, and with all the props needed to impress the customers.

Simmons was seated at a large desk over by the huge window—a small man, his white hair cropped close to give him a look of briskness and efficiency. He wore a light tan suit and, surprisingly, a dark blue shirt with a white tie. His face was deeply tanned and he was annoyed—annoyed and a little anxious.

"What can I do for you?" he asked, standing up as Minardi entered, but without introduction or handshake. Minardi flipped out his identification card, put it on the desk, selected a chair and sat without invitation. Simmons looked at the card and returned it to him, impatient. A detective in the Los Angeles Homicide Department didn't impress a man used to dealing with Central Intelligence and the FBI. Some of the anxiety left him, but the irritation mounted.

"You were a friend of Dr. Tighler's and saw him two days before his death," said Minardi. "What did you discuss with him?"

"It was entirely a social call. I can't remember that we discussed anything in particular."

"Did he seem worried—concerned—absent-minded?"

"No."

"How did he seem?"

"As usual."

"Entirely as usual?"

"Perhaps a little more bombastic, if that is the word, than usual. A little triumphant."

"Dr. Tighler was reckoned a security risk and so was not allowed employment on any government projects," said Minardi. "Was he working privately on anything?"

"Probably."

"Did he discuss with you anything that he was working on?"

"No."

"Dr. Smmons," said Minardi. "You're stalling. I'm dealing with a murder and an attempted murder. I want information."

"I am trying to give you information—to my considerable inconvenience," said Simmons.

"You are withholding information," said Minardi.

"I'm not some rookie cop inquiring into a traffic accident, so don't give me this stuff about two scientists meeting and talking trivialities to each other, and don't tell me that you don't know what Tighler was working on. That's a lie."

"A what?" said Simmons, his tanned faced flushing.

"A lie," said Minardi. "Your business is to keep abreast of scientific research of all kinds so as to service your clients. You could not afford not to know what Tighler was working on."

For reply Simmons reached across his desk as if to press a button and have Minardi escorted from the room. Then he changed his mind and said, "All right. I knew what Tighler was working on. But I don't know how far he had got with his work. I went to see him in the hope he would tell me something. He told me nothing, but I knew he had made a breakthrough."

"A breakthrough with what?"

"His project—nuclear vibration."

"Meaning what?" asked Minardi.

Simmons shrugged. "We haven't thoroughly assessed the potential and the application," he said. "Anything I say now would have to be in laymen's terms and therefore hugely misleading."

"Mislead me," said Minardi. "I'm not going to run off to the newspapers and give them a piece for the Sunday supplements."

"This is secret," said Simmons.

"I have a full clearance," said Minardi. "Go ahead."

"All right. In rough, inadequate and misleading terms, it's a method of splitting the atomic nucleus. Not to make a big bang, a new bomb. We have them so powerful now we don't need them any more. They're a waste of time. In fact, they are out of date. The atomic era lasted two bombs and a few experiments while everybody caught up and no more. We're far ahead of that. The real reason we got an effective ban on bomb testing with Russia was that there isn't any need for more tests. The weapon is out of date except for backward countries like China and France—scientifically backward," he added.

"What about this vibration stuff?"

"The old method of atom splitting was exactly that—splitting the nucleus apart by bombardment. Highly expensive, highly wasteful and hard to control. The method Tighler was working on—and some others, I might add—was one of . . . well, shaking the atom apart is the best way I can put it. You are familiar with the phenomenon of resonance?"

"Splintering a wine glass by playing a particular note on it?"

"Yes. The molecular adherence of the glass is weakened and it falls apart. Airplane wings do the same thing, as you will recall in the case of recent jet crashes, when a particular vibration is picked up, sets the molecular structure vibrating and the wing literally shakes to pieces. The point to remember is that this is merely molecular. The broken glass is still glass. The broken airplane wing is still steel and aluminum.

"But theoretically it is possible to do the same thing with the atomic nucleus, to discover the vibration of one of its particles and, by intensifying this, break the nucleus apart. Shake it apart. The atomic structure is then destroyed. There is a release of power—a tremendous release—and a regrouping of the particles to form a new element. It was on that that Tighler was working."

"Wouldn't he require tremendously expensive and elaborate apparatus for this kind of work?" asked Minardi.

"The Sunday comics," said Simmons. "Retorts, laser beams, photoelectric cells. Of course not. He required one piece of apparatus which he had himself—a magnificent brain. A trained brain. Like Einstein. The rest, the apparatus, is for mere technicians. All Einstein needed was his brain, and a pencil and paper. The rest grew out of that."

"Would this business be finally expressed in a mathematical formula—like Einstein's mass-energy formula?"

"Yes. Ultimately that would be inevitable. The logical conclusion would be a formula for the destruction of any atomic nucleus by that method. But before he got to that stage, Tighler would have had to undertake a tremendous amount of calculation from which to extract the necessary common factors." Simmons shrugged and gave a glance at the artificial heavens above him. "I find, actually, that I cannot explain this to you. The starting point is the Einstein mass-energy theorem. About midway you get the unified field on which Einstein had just finished work when he died. Further on, and I don't know how much further on (it may be further back) you get the Tighler problem."

"Was his work widely known?" asked Minardi.

"Not widely," said Simmons. "It was known of or suspected by top men in the field of mathematical theory. That's my field, by the way." Then, because he couldn't resist it, because he had had his work interrupted by this police detective and had been frightened a little by him, he said, "This office is one of my mathematical toys."

"A planetarium?" asked Minardi.

Simmons shook his head. "A toy illustrating celestial navigation light-years from earth," he said. "With it I can demonstrate the relative position of stars as seen from a rocket one hundred light-years from earth and headed to what we, on earth, would describe as the southeastern fringe of the Milky Way."

Minardi thought for a moment. "The stars are fixed in the sky," he said. "Is that really so difficult?"

"They are not fixed," said Simmons smugly. "They are moving at varying rates and speeds and in varying courses from a central point like fragments of an explosion, as Jeans demonstrated. They're not fixed at all." He paused. "Nothing on earth or in the heavens is fixed," he said. "There is nothing static and there are no vacuums. Everything is moving and everything contains something. There is no such quantity as nothing. Things appear static because we have not the instruments to detect their movement. Things appear empty because we have not the instruments to detect their content."

"Instruments?" asked the detective.

"Mathematics," said Simmons. "We were stuck for two thousand years with a mathematical system sufficient for the ancient Greeks. We struggled along with it, becoming increasingly aware that it was imperfect. It is only recently that we have started to expand it. The real advances in science are in mathematics. The rest is only a logical sequence emanating from new formula, new calculations. A mind, a sheet of paper, a pencil—that is the root of it all."

It was quite a little lecture, intended at one and the same time to instruct and to awe Minardi and put him in his place. But he wasn't awed.

"Where would your janitor fit in all of this?" he asked.

Simmons was completely taken aback. He reacted as if he had been winded by a blow in the stomach, and when he finally recovered, he said, "Janitor. What janitor?"

"Bodetkin. Paul Bodetkin."

"What of him?" he said. "He died. I don't understand what you mean."

"Forget it," said Minardi. "It was a heart attack. Let's get back to Tighler. There's solid ground there. He was murdered. I think you have given me the motive— whatever kind of formula he had worked out. You say he didn't seem afraid?"

"No." Simmons had lost his superiority, his inflated sense of ease.

"Mind if I look out your window?" asked Minardi.

"No. Not at all. Go ahead." Minardi went to the window. The room was on the first floor, with a planter of Palos Verdes stone outside, and beyond that an expanse of lawn with a high fence around. There was a fuse box near the fence, so Minardi guessed it was equipped with a burglar alarm. The main entrance road to Los Angeles International Airport skirted the fence, and he could see the flags of the different nations on the airport building.

Some flags weren't there, the flags of the nations which did not fly planes into the United States—the Soviet Union, Red China, Yugoslavia, Poland.

He turned to Simmons. "Tighler's formula, it goes without saying, would be of overwhelming interest to nations inimical to the United States," he said. "Let us suppose, putting aside what you call the Sunday comics, that he was the victim of espionage. Is it reasonable to presume that the killer was after the formula and would kill Tighler to prevent him passing it on to the United States government?"

Simmons hesitated before replying. "I will admit thinking of something like that myself," he said. "We've had the FBI here, Thomas Ralston. I would have thought you would be in touch with them."

"Go on," said Minardi. He didn't intend to explain the curious delicacies of the relationship between a local policing authority and the Federal Bureau of Investigation and its overseas cousin, the Central Intelligence Agency. He didn't know Thomas Ralston anyway, but it would be easy enough to get in touch with him if necessary. "Go on," Minardi repeated. "Would that be a reasonable action for an espionage agent—to kill Tighler?"

"For me that is unconvincing," said Simmons. "Too obvious, too clumsy. Even unnecessary. Wasteful. If they were after Tighler's formula—if he had a formula— there would be no need to kill Tighler."

"Except to prevent him passing the information on to his own government," said Minardi.

"Kidnaping would do that equally effectively—and

· *141*

also with Tighler alive, he would be of considerable use to his kidnapers. A brain like that isn't to be wiped out by mere murder. The whole thing is too clumsy."

Minardi thought that over. Clumsy was indeed the word for it. The impersonation of Father Bredder was clumsy. The attempt to make the impersonation stick by killing Father Bredder wasn't clumsy, except that it had failed. The device of officially clearing up one murder by another murder was daring but unskilled because of the possibilities of failure. There was no great intelligence behind these plans. He presumed that the agents of foreign powers were highly intelligent. But if such agents were involved, they had attempted something here that would have been turned down as impractical by a schoolboy.

"Are we dealing, when we talk of Tighler's formula, with something that could be expressed on one sheet of paper?" asked Minardi.

"Ultimately, yes," said Simmons. "But to be of any benefit, the steps leading to the formula itself would have to be explained. And that would run into sheet after sheet of highly involved mathematical calculation."

Minardi pulled a typewritten sheet from his jacket pocket, looked it over moodily and said, "I have here a list of known acquaintances of Dr. Tighler's. There are twenty-four men and eighteen women. The woman, according to our records, who was most often at his house is a Miss Brenda Albrecht. What do you know of her?"

"Tighler had his human side," said Simmons with a slight smile. "He had a great attraction for women and liked their company. Miss Albrecht was a close companion."

"How close?"

"I don't know. I am not a gossip columnist. He was a bachelor. She frequently acted as hostess for him when he entertained friends. She is a highly cultivated, intelligent woman and has been a friend of Dr. Tighler's for six or seven years."

Minardi grunted. "One more question," he said. "Why do you think Dr. Tighler was killed?"

"I haven't any idea."

"For his formula or over some personal matter?" Minardi persisted.

Simmons shrugged. *"Cherchez la femme,"* he said.

"Sunday comics," said Minardi to himself as he left.

Fifteen

MINARDI HAD one more call to make before going to see Miss Brenda Albrecht, whose address was given as Vista del Islas, Palos Verdes Estates. It was a call which he regarded as a waste of time, but because he was angry with Redwood, he decided to make it so that he could turn in a final report when the case was solved, so complete, so detailed, as to be a calculated rebuff to his chief.

He pulled into the parking area surrounding The Huddle café on the Pacific Coast Highway, pushed open the plate-glass and stainless steel door and sustained with a slight effort the thirty-degree change in temperature brought about by the air conditioning. There was a cashier's desk just before the door, with a service counter extending on both sides, with the usual stools for customers before it.

Beyond this counter was the kitchen, all aluminum and copper and arranged in such a way that the waitresses could talk directly to the cooks and the cooks, in handing out the food to the waitresses, were able to relieve the montoony of their work by a glance at the customer for whom the food was intended. Indeed, those cooks not employed on some order when Minardi entered were doing just that, leaning on the aluminum top of the counter across which they passed their orders, eyeing the customers and the waitresses. They had a good view of the restaurant and the street beyond.

Minardi perched himself on a stool and, swinging around on it so that his back was to the counter, surveyed the scene outside the windows. Any waitress or cook could see a car parked in front of the restaurant, which was what he wanted to check.

A waitress approached, gave him a glass of water and, after the manner of her kind, immediately went away. She returned and gave him a menu and was about to depart again, this being, in Minardi's experience, the inevitable behavior of waitresses in such places around Los Angeles. Minardi stopped her. "I wanted to speak to the manager," he said.

She picked up the menu and looked as if she was going to remove the glass of water. "We don't need any help," she said. She looked at him for the first time as a human being, appraising his experience and his need. He was middle-aged but he wasn't bad-looking. "Maybe they need someone in the kitchen," she said.

"I'm not looking for a job," said Minardi.

"You'll have to see Miss Stebbins about the manager," said the waitress. "We do all our ordering on the phone. Five o'clock."

"Thanks," said Minardi. "Is Miss Stebbins the cashier?"

"Yes," said the waitress. She hesitated. "If you're from the egg people, get ready to duck," she said. "They're real mad about that short delivery this morning."

"Thanks," said Minardi, and moved over to the cashier. This time he produced his identification. She started when she read the card. It was the reaction of the innocent. The guilty train themselves to look unimpressed.

"I want to see the manager," he said, and she replied quickly, "Yes, sir," and took him immediately to an office at the end of the restaurant, beyond the rest rooms. She pushed open the door without knocking and said, "Mr. Williams. There's a policeman to see you." Then she fled to spread the news to the waitresses and the cooks.

Williams was a thin, pinched, nervous man in his early thirties, with thinning fair hair and the look of a sufferer from prolonged indigestion. His office was an untidy collection of odds and ends of tubular furniture, the cast-offs of other restaurants. His desk was a mere piece of plywood on tubular legs, and was littered with papers. There were two telephones on it, their tangled cords giving evidence of much hasty use. Part of the office was used for the storage of bottles of syrup, some empty and others half full. Williams might be the manager, but he looked like the kind of manager who was harried to the limit of endurance by his staff. He was very nervous.

"What time do you open in the morning?" asked Minardi.

"Eight o'clock, sir," said the manager.

"Your staff would start arriving about seven?"

"Yes."

"Do you have blinds on those front windows which are lowered at night?"

"No, sir. We leave lights on in the restaurant at night

and the blinds up. As an added protection against burglary."

Minardi nodded. It was a usual procedure and a good one for such places.

"On August 8th, a man was reported as dead of a heart attack in a car which pulled up in front of this restaurant," he said. "Name of Bodetkin. Paul Bodetkin."

"Yes. But I wasn't on duty then. That was a Tuesday. I get Mondays and Tuesdays off. The assistant manager was on. He's away today."

"It doesn't matter," said Minardi. "Who was serving behind the counter? Who were the cooks? Who was the cashier that day?"

Williams fumbled among the papers on his desk without effect, opened two drawers in quick succession, and then went to a battered filing cabinet. This he opened and started pawing through some folders. Eventually he returned to his desk, pressed a button and the cashier, Miss Stebbins, appeared.

"This is Lieutenant Minardi of the police," said Williams. "He wants to know who was on duty when the man was found dead in the car. I can't find the lists."

"I have them to make up the payroll," said Miss Stebbins. She gave a nervous look at Minardi. "We pay every other week," she said. "That's why I have them."

"Fine," said Minardi. "Can you bring into the office here the various people who were on duty that day? Let's start with you. Were you on duty?"

"Yes." Her voice had a tremble in it and Minardi felt sorry for her.

"Nothing to be frightened of, Miss Stebbins," he said. "This is just a routine investigation. Our records aren't quite complete."

"Oh," she said. "I just don't like getting mixed up with police."

"Nobody does," said Minardi. "Were you at work on time that morning?"

She looked anxiously at Williams and said, "No. I was fifteen minutes late." She turned to Williams. "I entered that on my time card," she said. "My car wouldn't start."

"That's quite all right," said Williams.

"So you would have arrived at quarter past seven?"

"Yes."

"Did you see a car parked out in front of the restaurant when you arrived?"

"No."

"Would you have noticed a car if one was there?"

"Yes. I think so. It's a limited parking area—fifteen minutes. It isn't usual for people to park there."

"After you arrived, did you notice a car parked there—with a man in it?"

"I saw a car. But I couldn't see a man in it." That checked. Bodetkin was slumped across the front seat when found.

"When was that?"

"A little after eight. About eight-fifteen."

The others who were questioned, two waitresses and a dishwasher, confirmed this account. Those who had seen the car had seen it not earlier than about eight-fifteen. Minardi had to wait for half an hour for the cook who had been on duty that morning to report for work. He had worked the day shift that week and was on the swing shift now.

He was a big, loosely built man, pasty-faced and with the look of a hard drinker. When he came into Williams' office, he pulled a crate of bottles away from the wall and sat on it with a kind of contempt for the manager.

"Sure I remember," he said. "We had everything ready to go at eight and I opened up the hatches and about fifteen minutes later this guy came in and gave me the first order—Number Three, over easy."

"Choice of orange or grape juice, two ranch eggs with ham or bacon, two golden waffles and coffee," said Williams.

"What guy?" asked Minardi.

"The first guy to order breakfast that day," said the cook. "I always remember the first. Big guy. Wore a dark suit that was a bit mussed up and sat over in the corner."

"Was the car there?" asked Minardi.

"Right. I told Esther when I gave her the order to tell the guy to move the car because it was in a fifteen-minute zone. He said it wasn't his car."

"Did he have a car?"

"No. He came walking."

"Did he have anything with him?"

"He had one of them cases people carry papers in. He put it on the table. I noticed that because most of them put it beside the table and then forget it when they leave. But he put it on the table. Then I got busy and didn't notice anything more."

"That was about quarter past eight?"

"Right."

"How do you know he didn't have a car? He might have parked it in the proper parking area behind the restaurant."

"Because he said he didn't have a car. Why would he lie abut it?" asked the chef. There was no air conditioning in Mr. Williams' storeroom office, and he was beginning to sweat a little, the water glistening on his pasty, drinker's face. He got up off the crate, pulled out a bottle, took the top off it and started drinking the contents, warm as they were.

"Good for what ails you," he said. "Mostly whisky," and he winked at Minardi.

"Give me as good a description as you can of this man," said Minardi.

"Well, big—six foot, I'd say. Close-cut hair. Kind of blocky face and hands. Dark suit, rumpled like I said. His shirt was clean but rumpled a bit, and the knot on his tie was pulled real tight so the tie didn't sit right. Cheapskate. Left a ten-cent tip. That Number Three costs a dollar forty-five."

"You say he had on a dark kind of suit. Was it heavy material?" asked Minardi.

"Not real heavy. But he wasn't from Los Angeles."

"Why do you say that?"

"People don't wear dark suits here," said the chef. "San Francisco, yes. I worked up there for years. All dark suits. Los Angeles is light-colored suits. More sun. I figure he was off a plane and had come up here looking for breakfast."

"Long way to walk for breakfast," said Minardi.

"About two miles. And there are restaurants at the airport."

"Try and get some service in them," said the cook. "Takes half an hour to get a cup of coffee. I know. I worked there. Probably took a taxi at the airport, stopped here and got some breakfast."

"Did you see a taxi?"

"No."

"Did you see the man enter the restaurant?"

"Yes. Came in the front door—not that side one. About that taxi. Coming from the airport, it would have either to make a U-turn or drop him off across the road."

"That's true," said Minardi.

He wanted to find out one thing further and got that from the dishwasher. The dishwasher's chores included hosing down the parking area around the restaurant first thing in the morning. He had done so that day as usual and had seen no car in the area before eight-twenty.

When he left, Minardi drove to headquarters in deep thought and called Auto Theft. "Have you any reports of cars stolen in the Westchester area August 8th?" he asked. It was a long shot and he had to wait a while for the answer.

"We have a report of a nineteen forty-six Chevrolet convertible stolen from the Broadway Department store. Reported at ten A.M. Let's see. Yes, the car was found wrecked at the foot of the cliffs at Lunada Bay."

"Fingerprints?"

"Owner's on the door and seat, and so on. Seats were naugahyde. Others not so good, but nothing on them. We figured some kid on a morning spree."

"Okay," said Minardi. "Thanks. Listen. Do me a favor. I've got more than I can handle. Call Identification and ask them to go over that car inch by inch and get every fingerprint they can off of it. I know it's been out in the weather for two weeks, but this is special. Remember, everything they can find. Did it catch fire when it hit the bottom of the cliff?"

"No."

"Good." Minardi put down the phone. He was tingling with excitement when he called Simms, the pathologist.

"Paul Bodetkin. Heart attack," he said. "Number"—he looked it up—"88 HA 245. How precise can you be on the hour of death?"

"He had been dead no more than three hours when examined. That's the limit."

"When was the examination?"

"Ten in the morning."

"So he could have been dead at seven?"

"Yes. That's possible."

"Can you be sure of that—sure enough for a judge and jury?"

"Oh, yes. Kissler did a lot of work on it. It can be readily demonstrated by coagulation and temperature. Child's play."

"Did the post-mortem indicate that Bodetkin had had heart trouble previously?"

"Ummmmmmmm," said Simms, and Minardi could visualize him pulling at his long nose as he always did in thought. "There was hardening of some of the arteries, a little enlargement of the heart muscles. He had heart damage, but minor. The attack itself was classical angina pectoris—a very large clot of blood lodged in the aorta. Strychnine injected directly into the heart would have been the old remedy, and might have worked had it been

152 ·

done right away. Produces a massive convulsion, you know."

"Seven o'clock, then? That's the limit. Thanks a lot."

He hung up and looked thoughtfully at the folder on Paul Bodetkin. Next to his name were the words "Heart Attack Victim." Minardi lightly penciled through the words "Heart attack" and wrote instead the one word "Murder." He thought a moment and placed a question mark after the word.

Sixteen

"IT'S GOING to be real dark down there, and wrecks are dangerous," said Bob Meistrell. "I shouldn't really be doing this. You ought to make your first ocean dive in about twenty feet of clear water on a sunny day. Like at Cherry Cove. That's where we check out all our divers."

"I'm not really interested in becoming a diver," said Father Bredder. "I just want to go down on that barge. I want to look around it. And after that I probably won't ever dive again."

He had been given four days of intensive scuba diving instructions by Bob and Billy and the fact that Father Bredder was taking such instruction had created quite a little stir among divers in what is loosely called the South Bay. There had been an item about it in the *Daily Breeze,* the community newspaper, with a picture, and the reporter had noted that Father Bredder was to dive on the sunken barge lying in seventy-five feet of water near Palos Verdes Point.

Father Bredder was quite pleased with the item, which was unusual for him, for he didn't like publicity, and he was especially pleased that the little story had mentioned the date and time on which he was to make his dive.

"Father Bredder, priest of the Roman Catholic Church and noted amateur detective," the report read "reflects the point of view of many ministers of different faiths that these days the clergy must take part in the activities of their flock. His interest in diving has been further stimulated by the fact that he and Lieutenant Minardi of the Los Angeles Police Force were the ones who discovered the body of a drowned scuba diver, identified as Philip Norwood, while fishing off the Hermosa Beach Pier a few weeks ago."

That was good enough bait, the priest reflected, and he recalled the words of Minardi when they had been fishing off the pier that day. "Fishing," Minardi had said, "calls for the exercise of two of the cardinal virtues—Prudence and Fortitude." He reflected that there wasn't much prudence about the kind of fishing he was doing, and perhaps an excess of fortitude. He trusted that it really was fortitude and not presumption, which, far from being one of the cardinal virtues, was one of the deadly sins.

The *Linda Kay* plowed in the dying day toward Palos Verdes Point, and the priest, clad from head to toe in a thick neoprene rubber suit, still could not get accustomed to the clumsiness he felt. He seemed off balance. When he moved his arms and legs, it was awkwardly and slowly, as if they didn't really belong to him or perhaps as if he was moving them in one of those terrible dreams, where the actions of self-defense, of striking or of running are frighteningly slow and futile. Bob Meistrell moved with much more assurance and speed, though similarly clad. His diving suit was old and patched at the knees and the elbows. That, the priest knew, was from work underwater, kneeling on rocks and coral, working with outfall pipes, two hundred feet below the surface in a remote and highly hostile world.

His twin Bill, also clad in a wetsuit, was at the controls, headed for the point which they were approaching swiftly. He throttled down, headed into the seas at idling speed and called, "Bobby—do you see the oil?"

"You're way off," said Bobby, glancing at the shoreline. "About two hundred yards more."

"No, I'm not. It should be right here."

"Billy. Don't you remember your line-up? The old bridge of the *Dominator* with that white house on the cliff?"

"No, I don't remember. The last time we were here you said it was that black rock and the ravine right behind."

"That's the lobster spot," said Bob. "Don't you ever get anything right? Here, give me the wheel."

"I can steer," said Billy. "Just tell me where we're supposed to go. And you'd better be quick. It's getting so dark we won't see the oil." The twins finally settled for a new line-up altogether, involving a patch of white cliff and the stern section of the wrecked Liberty vessel, *Dominator*.

"There's the oil," said Bill. "Get the anchor." Bob already had his weight belt and tank on and, though monstrously encumbered by those two items, moved with agility and let the *Linda Kay's* anchor over as soon as the launch was dead in the water. As soon as he heard the anchor splash, he started to move the *Linda Kay* slowly astern so the chain wouldn't foul the hook, and when he felt it was set, killed the engine. Then he went forward and stared at the anchor chain going down into the depths and looked at the heaving ocean around.

"Bit of a swell," he said. "But it won't bother you on the wreck. I think the anchor's just ten feet off her on the starboard side."

"You'd better be right," said Bob, helping Father Bredder into his gear. "Better get your tank on."

"I'm not diving," said Billy. "I'll stay here and watch the *Linda Kay*. I don't like this surface swell."

There was another argument, but Billy won.

The weight belt, twenty pounds of lead because he was such a big man, made Father Bredder feel that he was cut in two from the waist down, the lower half of him ponderous, the upper half still agile. This was remedied when Bob put the dive tank on his back, reuniting his whole body in clumsiness. His balance was so bad that the slight rocking of the launch made him stumble and he had to brace his big feet well apart to keep his balance.

Left to himself, it would probably have taken him half an hour to get all his gear on—the weight belt, the tank, the regulator, an inflatable jacket called a Mae West, a knife strapped around his leg, his swin fins, his face plate, gloves, and then an underwater flashlight thrust into his hand and tied to him by a piece of string wrapped around his wrist. The thought occurred to him that with all this equipment he would certainly drown. As soon as he was over the side, he would sink like a broken and weighted crab to the gloomy bottom below, incapable of making any effective effort to save himself.

He put the faceplate over his nose and eyes and the regulator in his mouth and took a suck of the air. It tasted of rubber, as it had done during the lessons in the swimming pool—moist fresh rubber.

"We'll go down the anchor chain, Father," said Bob. "Take it real easy. If your ears hurt, stop, come up a little and clear them by pinching your nose and blowing into it. Don't keep going down if they hurt. You'll bust an eardrum. Okay?"

The priest nodded.

"Another thing—stay close to me. We won't be able to see much more than four or five feet down there. And don't panic. Above all, don't hold your breath. Keep breathing. All the time. Okay?"

Father Bredder nodded again. Bob checked his gear over item by item, sat on the side of the cockpit with his back to the water and rolled overboard, his hand clapped over his faceplate. Father Bredder suspected that if he waited for Bob to surface, he might have difficulty getting up enough nerve to do the same thing. Diving in a swimming pool in ten feet of water was a far different matter from diving into the ocean at seventy feet. So he turned his big back to the ocean, plumped down on the cockpit, swung his feet up into the air and hit the water with a mighty splash. When he opened his eyes, he was upside down in an explosion of small green bubbles, all sense of direction gone except for the impression that his legs were above his head.

He rolled over, felt a slight weight on his back, raised his head and found he was on the surface and just afloat. Bob swam over to him and led him to the anchor chain.

They stayed there a moment while Father Bredder recovered from the shock of the dive and took some comforting sucks of air from the regulator, breathing rather faster than normal, for he couldn't quite assure his panicked lungs that there actually was air available.

Bob, holding the anchor chain, took his regulator out of his mouth and said, "I'll go first. Real slow. Start clearing as soon as your head is under the water."

He turned, grabbed the chain, upended himself so that his flippers appeared for a brief moment rather like the flukes of a very small whale, and then he was gone. The priest made no attempt at so graceful a descent. He just grabbed the anchor chain and started pulling himself down after Bob. For a few seconds he felt dizzy and wondered whether his air was all right. He remembered snatches of conversation among divers about oil getting into the air, or exhaust fumes, and causing sickness. Then he realized that he was actually standing on his head, and the dizziness was the result of this unusual posture. When he recognized the cause, the dizziness went.

Ahead of him in the dwindling light, the anchor chain extended down into nothingness. He could see only twenty links or so, and beyond them the graceful undulation of Bob's flippers. The links slipped up to him out of nothingness, passed him, and went on into nothingness. He thought of the old Saxon chieftain who had seen in this the summary of man's life on earth—coming from nowhere and going to nowhere. But for the Saxon chief it had been a swallow which had flown out of the darkness into his tent and out into the darkness again. And for

Father Bredder it was the chain, each link a day or a month or a year, coming from eternity, slipping into eternity. The concept comforted him rather than frightened him, however. Eternity was the reality and the present not an illusion but a mere shadow or distorted reflection of that reality.

There was a slight wedging sensation in his right ear. He stopped, put one hand against his nostrils, pressing them shut through the rubber rim of the faceplate and exhaled hard through his nose. The wedging was slightly relieved. He swallowed and there was a tremendous squeak in the inner ear, and the wedging sensation was gone. Bob had turned and come up to him. He held out thumb and forefinger in a circle, asking the diver's question, "Okay?" Father Bredder pointed to his right ear and then, making a circle of thumb and forefinger, indicated all was well. They continued downward.

It was time now to look about and to listen. This was no silent world the priest found himself in. It was filled with the noise of his own breathing; a hissing, whistling, bubbling tumult more intimate and urgent than anything he had heard on land. Not a silent world at all, but a watching world, teeming with eyes all fixed on him— ultramicroscopic sense organs of billions of diatoms scarcely to be called eyes and one immense optic which was the sum total of all these others. The edges of the world lay four feet ahead and around him and beyond that was eternity, watching him.

Suddenly, reaching his hand ahead to pull himself down the anchor chain, he plunged into icy coldness. The temperature change was so sharp he started. A thermocline. Warm water above and cold water below and not a fraction of an inch separating the two layers. He went on down into this frigidity, and the quality of the light changed.

Above, the light had been greenish, like the filterings of the sun through poisonous fog. Now the light was less but clear—a clear darkness. He switched on the underwater flashlight and it threw its beam fifteen feet well ahead of Bob. Fewer diatoms here. This was too cold for them. He was in dead water, in crystal ice-cold darkness, and eternity was either farther away or very much closer. He couldn't decide which. Bob turned and shone his flashlight on him, avoiding the priest's eyes so as not to dazzle him. Again he questioned "Okay?" with his fingers, and the priest replied in kind.

He felt heavy now, and knew they were very much deeper. Nearer the surface he had had to pull himself down the chain; now he started to sink, the chain slipping between his fingers. He even had to brake himself so as not to go too fast. And then, to his astonishment, something came out of the nothingness ahead—a solid blurred something with white specks on it, and he was on the bottom.

It was, strangely, a little clearer here. Even without the flashlight he could see Bob, the white of his gloves, the white rubber around his faceplate, and the shine of the stainless steel buckles on his weight belt and tank harness. The tank was visible, too, a subdued gray cylinder, but the dark suit was sensed rather than seen.

Bob turned to him and he could scarcely distinguish his features in the shadows behind the faceplate. He jerked with his thumb to their left, and the priest followed him, swimming clumsily along the bottom and so overweighted now that he had to push himself up several times off the ooze and sand.

They went only a few feet and a dark cliff mournfully clad in tattered roses and vile weed rose before them— the wreck of a ghastly castle perhaps from some Gothic tale. But it was the barge, festooned with pink and red sea anemones and thin primitive strings of slime, with here and there some branchlike thing growing from the sides like a leafless shrub.

Bob reached the barge first, indicated that they were to swim to the deck twenty feet above them, and pushed off from the bottom.

He swam with his feet alone, his hands trailing at his sides, but Father Bredder used his arms in a clumsy breaststroke and, before gaining the deck of the barge, and stirred up a great cloud of sand and ooze. It was a few seconds before this settled down and they could see about them.

They were on the top deck of the barge, whose sides and extremities were invisible. The deck was covered with growth. At Father Bredder's feet was some kind of deck fitting like an overturned saucer, covered with shells and moss. He reached to pick it up. It shrunk a little and scuttled off to a gloomy corner. It turned out to be a crab.

Bob gestured and swam toward what the priest guessed was the bow of the barge, for he had said he wanted to inspect that area, but he had to go down through the forward hatch. Father Bredder swam after him, pushing himself along the deck with his hands, for his swimming was clumsy, but he was careful not to touch any of the fittings. Bob stopped and turned his flashlight to a ventilator cowl. Two evil heads peered out of it, mouthing and undulating, like maggots caught in sliced cheese. Moray eels. They stared at the priest as he went by, but made no move toward him.

Suddenly they were beside the forward hatch, which lay open, the hatch cover smashed and tumbled to one side. A length of heavy rusty chain was reared out of the hatch and tumbled about the deck nearby, like some stricken serpent of mythology. Bob turned to the priest and, holding both hands with the fingers outstretched, pushed them toward him twice. They had been over these signals. This signal meant he was to stay there for a moment. Bob would be back. The priest nodded, for this was as he had planned. He lay on the deck on his stomach, peering down into the hatch into which Bob disappeared. It was utterly black down there—the black of the abyss. He saw the flashing beam move around and then it was gone, extinguished in a moment, and a feeling of utter loneliness and of dread expectation overwhelmed the priest.

He lay then where he was, tense, aware of his own breathing and the increasing cold and the moray eels in the ventilator and the crabs scuttling about in the gloom—crabs which, assisted by limpets, barnacles and other patient destroyers, would in time gnaw this huge wreck to nothing.

After a little time he both felt and heard a movement below in the lower hold. The sound was a metallic one like the chiming of a bell, and the movement was a displacement of water washing suddenly up the hatch toward him. He became increasingly alert. He shone his flashlight down into the hold and saw bubbles coming through the rotted flooring from below. He deliberately continued this attitude of staring into the hold, waiting for what he believed would happen. He watched the bubbles coming up between the planks in little silvery curtains, clean and delightful and in sharp contrast to the moldering ruin around.

He was anxious to get down into the hold himself to search for what he had come for which instinct rather than reason had told him was somewhere aboard the wreck. It would be in a watertight box, and the box would be concealed, so the search might be long. But it was necessary to wait here, alone, first.

While he was still looking into the hold, something touched him on the shoulder and he looked up and saw a figure above him. The diver swam over his head, then dived down into the hatch. Father Bredder followed. He didn't swim into the hatch himself so much as sink into it, for he was not the best of swimmers and he still found the neoprene wetsuit cumbersome. He followed from the upper hold into the lower one and here the darkness was total, pierced only by the narrow beam of his flashlight.

Suddenly the other's flashlight went out. The priest had been half expecting this, and knew what to do. He was kneeling on the floor of the lower hatch and shone the light above and about him. He picked up the other diver, over his head, shone the light directly into his face and knew from the dark faceplate that the diver was not Bob, but the one he suspected would come for him.

He switched off the flashlight immediately and moved aside, though clumsily. He did not move fast enough. He felt arms grab him, and his faceplate was ripped off in a second so that even if he had used the flashlight, he would be completely blind now. He struggled, fighting, as it were, an octopus in the dark.

The other diver was still behind and above him, fumbling with his tank while the priest struggled to free himself from his grasp. The diver was not so much powerful as quick and expert. He cut off the priest's air and in the same movement snatched the regulator from his mouth so that all the air he had was that which remained in his lungs from his last breath.

He had been pinned down on his stomach, but now managed to roll over. A hand was clasped over his face, thumb and forefinger pinching his nostrils shut and the palm sealing his mouth closed so that he could not breathe out.

Father Bredder had reasoned out ahead of the dive the likely course of the attack if it came. The next move would be to undo his weight belt and swim him upward while still sealing the air in his lungs. The pressure of the sealed air would swell his lungs like a balloon as he went upward. The lungs would rip and he would be killed by air embolism, in the same way as Philip Norwood had been killed.

He tried to kick his attacker off with his feet but kept catching his flippers on the chain on the bottom of the hold. The chain gave him an idea. It stretched from this lower hold to the deck above and was somewhere over to his right. He reached for it, felt its barnacle-encrusted links, and heaved. The other diver was still over him, fumbling for the release buckle on his weight belt.

Father Bredder managed to get one foot under the chain that lay on the floor for purchase and heaved again, and this time the chain above gave. It came down slowly at first, only an inch or two, and then picked up speed. The priest, exerting all his strength, flung himself aside and free of his attacker and the chain came thundering down in a Niagara, the sound as heavy as a cannonade. Several loops fell over him, pinning him to the deck, but the main body fell on the diver who had attacked him.

His lungs were now bursting for air. He swallowed and achieved a measure of relief and forced himself to think calmly. The first thing to do was get his air supply turned on again. He reached back, found the valve and turned it. He got the regulator hose and pulled it down and put the mouthpiece between his teeth and sucked hungrily. The relief was immense.

Without a faceplate, he still could not see, but this did not bother him greatly. He had the combat veteran's ability to work by feel, and he knew that the first thing he had to do was get out from underneath the several loops of chain that had fallen on him. He worked away at this and forced himself to open his eyes while he did so.

He got his feet out of the flippers and saw a blurry light some distance off. It was quickly right next to him and he held up his hands to ward off an attack. But no attack came. Instead a faceplate was thrust into his hand and he put it on and cleared it of water as Bob had instructed him during the diving lessons in the pool. Then the flashlight was handed to him and in the beam he saw Bob, who had removed his own faceplate to give it to the priest.

Bob then did something very curious. He put his hands over his forehead, the fingers linked to form a kind of visor, and exhaled some air so that it was trapped by the visor of the fingers. He then started swimming very slowly over the hold. He went over to the other side of the mound of chain, disappeared and, when he returned, he had the priest's faceplate on.

There were bubbles coming from the heap of chain, and the two started to pull the chain aside. They found first the hand of the diver and then the head. His regulator was not in his mouth. Bob put it in between his teeth, clamped his jaw shut on it, and they got him free of the chain. Then Bob grabbed him from behind around the chest and started up with him, squeezing hard to expel the air from his lungs as they went. He dropped the unconscious diver's weight belt to make the ascent quicker, and Father Bredder followed him up.

When they reached the surface, they were some distance from the *Linda Kay*. Bob took out his regulator and shouted to Bill to come for them. The launch sped over and they got the diver aboard. Bill started mouth-to-mouth resuscitation, pulling off the diver's hood to get his jaws open more readily. When he did so, a mass of damp blond hair tumbled out, and the twins looked at each other in surprise. Father Bredder remembered the diver with the high-pitched voice who had tried to drown him in Avalon Bay.

Seventeen

"YOU WERE quite right," said Lieutenant Minardi. "I was goofing on the job. Maybe if you hadn't assigned me to that Bodetkin death but called me in when Tighler was murdered, I'd have done better. But I just couldn't take seriously an investigation of a man—a janitor—who had been medically certified as having died of a heart attack.

"We know now that the heart attack occurred during an attempt at murder. But I wouldn't have found that out if you hadn't angered me."

"That's why I angered you," said Redwood. "Every man has his tender spot. Yours is your professional reputation. Mine is that I hate pretenses and artificialities. Run over the whole case for me briefly and tell me where we stand right now. This isn't the only murder in Los Angeles, you know. I have other things on my mind." Minardi recognized the prod as a goad to keep him on his toes, but he was in a repentful mood and didn't resent it.

"We'll start with Bodetkin," said Minardi. "He was a janitor at Intersystems. He had held that job for five years—since the company was founded. He was thoroughly investigated before being cleared for the work and had a good record, including something I should have given special attention to—namely, war service with Army Intelligence in their cipher department. He was an expert at breaking codes or making codes. I've talked to our own people about this and they tell me that the perfect code uses material which is readily available to anyone and is entirely innocent except when examined through the key.

"In Bodetkin's case he used books and sheet music. There were two stages. The first was to encode certain information using selected words from pages of specific books. The letters of the words were given a numerical value. For instance, the letter "c" at the beginning of a word on page ten would be three to the power of ten. Whatever that answer was, and I'm only giving you an example, was expressed algebraically by a symbol, and then the symbol put into a musical code. Suppose the symbol allotted was 'x.' It was referred to sheet music and expressed perhaps as B-flat."

"As far as I am aware," said Redwood, "there are only thirteen semitones in our scale. Wouldn't that be a bit limiting?"

"Not the way music is written," said Minardi. "B-flat can actually be written A-sharp, when it would have a different value in the code. Then you can get into double flats and double sharps, so the range is pretty wide, and a very complicated algebraic formula can be expressed in a few bars of music and appear perfectly innocent except to a skilled musician."

"I suppose it would play rather queer," said Redwood,

"but these days, most music does. Who suggested this line of investigation?"

"Father Bredder," said Minardi.

"He is a skilled musician?"

"No. But he noted that there were negatives of music manuscript in Bodetkin's darkroom on the same piece of film and written in two keys which did not agree. He suspected that it was music not used as music. He calls that kind of reasoning 'Recognizing Spiritual Fingerprints.' "

"Spiritual hogwash," snorted Redwood.

"Hogwash for us, sir," said Minardi. "But not for Father Bredder. Those spiritual fingerprints of his led him to suspect the existence of the whole ciphering system just from examining the contents of Bodetkin's room and Tighler's study—the oddity of music not used as music and books not read as books. He was way ahead of us there."

"What do you mean 'books not read as books'?" asked Redwood. "How could he tell whether they were read as books or not?"

"It's a little difficult to explain because with Father Bredder it is a feeling," said Minardi. "But basically he says that people who like books tend to read certain kinds of books and avoid other kinds. That is their spiritual attitude toward books, and it's corroborated by booksellers, who become experts in the tastes of particular customers. But both Tighler's and Bodetkin's collection of books showed no particular taste. Then in Bodetkin's case there was the music in two unrelated keys without modulation, which was wrong. It was music not to be used as music."

Redwood turned in his chair to face the window, as was his habit when his thinking was disturbed, saw the hated palm tree and turned back.

"And this dive business of his," he said. "I'm glad nothing has got into the papers about it yet, other than that he made a dive on that wreck. But where does that fit in?"

"I'd sooner stick to Bodetkin for the time being," said Minardi. "He will lead us to the wreck. He was encoding information summarizing Tighler's findings on atomic resonance. The whole formula was expressed musically, photographed and put in a watertight capsule and hidden —not on land but in the sea. In that wrecked barge, in fact; under the pile of chain in the lower hold. We passed the capsule on to the FBI, as you know."

"I know," said Redwood. "Go on."

"Bodetkin was not himself a diver," said Minardi, "and it is possible that he would have settled for hiding the capsule somewhere on land. A bank vault, safety deposit box, any place like that would have been good enough in ordinary circumstances. But these were not ordinary circumstances. Tighler knew there were others after his formula—his equation—and he wanted a hiding place completely novel and completely secure. Even bank officials can be got to when the stakes are high enough. He was a remarkable man—a highly trained mind but, unlike many highly trained minds, capable of vigorous imagination. It was probably he who thought of hiding the capsule in the ocean, and we have a link between him and Philip Norwood.

"Norwood was a student of Tighler's ten years ago when he lectured on mathematics at Caltech. Norwood was a diver. Tighler trusted him and, after some conversations of which we will never know anything, charged him to find a hiding place for the capsule in the ocean. He chose the wrecked barge with the heap of chain in its forepeak."

"Not a good choice, in my view," said Redwood. "Surely there was some danger of a diver deciding to salvage the chain?"

"No, sir," said Minardi. "The barge had been on the bottom for a year at that time. Divers had stripped it already of anything salvageable. The chain was encrusted with growth and heavily rusted. It would not be worth the labor of moving it. But to go on. Bodetkin has led us to Tighler and to Norwood.

"Norwood turned up drowned—or rather dead of air embolism, which could be an accident or could be murder. It was after that item appeared in the papers that Tighler called Father Bredder. He was quite right when he said he wanted to talk to Father Bredder about a matter involving national security. He suspected that Norwood had been murdered. When Bodetkin was found dead in his car of a heart attack, his suspicions were aggravated. He thought he might be next on the list and called the priest, who told him to go to others, since it was not a matter of spiritual assistance.

"Later, someone impersonating Father Bredder called him back and said he would visit him, and an appointment was made. That person arrived disguised as the priest, was admitted by the housekeeper and killed Tighler."

"Wait a minute," said Redwood. "There's a lot in

there that isn't right. How did the murderer know that Tighler had called Father Bredder in the first place?"

"He made the call while Brenda Albrecht was with him. She's confessed to that."

"And this other person, the killer, did she name him?"

"Yes. But she didn't really have to. The FBI and Central Intelligence are already on his trail. They have his fingerprints. He should be picked up soon."

"His fingerprints? How did they get them?"

A blush showed on Minardi's face, despite his shallow olive complexion.

"I had them all the time, sir," he said. "I got them on a booklet of matches in Marty's Café. I'd forgotten about them. It was only when I started going over all the details, everything that happened, that I remembered the matches. Three excellent prints of thumb, middle and forefinger of the right hand. Jimmy Headley, alias Jim Head, alias Tom Penston, whose real name is Angelo Corbini; illegal immigrant from Italy, twice deported, three times returned, wanted on a whole list of charges from narcotics through attempted murder. A professional hoodlum. One interesting item about him, he had a Dishonorable Discharge from the Italian Navy, where he was one of the early frogmen."

"And who was employing him?"

Minardi recalled the scene in Simmons' office when he had looked out at the International Airport and the flags of all the nations flying over the administration building in the westerly wind. He thought of the flags of the nations which were not represented in that display of international communication and he said flatly, "The FBI merely say 'The Others.' "

Redwood grunted. He was a policeman. When it came to "The Others," that wasn't his job. "They picked a pretty clumsy operator," he commented.

Minardi nodded. "It was a rough kind of job, anyway," he said. "All they needed was Tighler dead."

"Why dead?" asked Redwood. "Surely he was more valuable alive."

Minardi did not reply immediately because he needed to find the words with which to express himself without sensationalism. "This formula of Tighler's—roughly called atomic resonance," he said, "was something by which the world could be shaken apart. Tighler had it and they hadn't. They suspected it's hiding place, however—the hiding place both of the formula and the key to decoding it. They murdered Norwood, Corbini being the murderer. If Tighler was also killed, then they had the formula exclusively, with no prospect of it being rediscovered in this country for some years. With such a weapon at their disposal they could work their will with us."

"Just how was Tighler suffocated?" asked Redwood. "How could that be done without a single bruise on him?"

"Neoprene rubber—the diver's material," said Minardi. "The murderer came in dressed as a priest and the physical resemblance, as far as size was concerned, was enough to deceive the housekeeper. He was admitted to Tighler's study. Remember Tighler had never met Father Bredder and didn't know what he looked like. All the murderer had to do was pull a gun, tie Tighler up with strips of neoprene which wouldn't bruise, gag him, perhaps, and then put one of those cellophane bags over his head. He'd be dead in a very few minutes."

"Cellophane bags?" questioned Redwood. "Was that what was used?"

"It's a guess. But Father Bredder says that divers use them all the time to collect shells, and so forth, and they even trap live fish in them. It's a natural diver's tool and the kind of thing Corbini, himself a veteran diver, would use. A spiritual fingerprint, Father Bredder would say."

"And Brenda Albrecht?"

"The old story. Living too high, a friend of Tighler's, offered money for seemingly innocent information until she was in so deep and was so scared that murder was the only way out. Actually two attempted murders, with Father Bredder the intended victim on both occasions. She was the one who was driving the launch during the first attempt at Catalina—the diver with the boyish voice."

"It's a wonder that Corbini himself didn't attempt to kill Father Bredder on the barge," said Redwood. "He's the professional. Why send the Albrecht woman?"

"Because he's a professional," said Minardi. "He suspected a trap in the prior newspaper publicity. He sent her to do the dirty work, perhaps intending that if she failed, she would be blamed for everything. He has a curious clumsiness that way."

"And our old friend Shiny?"

"He was at the Hermosa Pier by sheer coincidence," said Minardi. "I've spoken to him and got whatever kind of confession you can get out of a guy like Shiny. Being there when we found Norwood's body proved valuable. Corbini needed someone to keep a tag on me and Father Bredder, and he used Shiny. In Catalina he was to warn Corbini if I was with Father Bredder when he came down for his appointment on the pier. He was to create a row with me when the attempt on Father Bredder would be put off."

"That's complicity to commit a murder," said Redwood.

"It is," said Minardi. "Or it would be if you were dealing with anyone of intelligence. But Shiny's brain has gone a little soft. Too much alcohol. He'll do anything he's asked without considering whether it is right or wrong, providing the reward is sufficient."

"Write this whole thing up and get hold of Shiny and send him to me," said Redwood.

When Shiny appeared, Redwood said, "I could put you away for life for complicity in a murder plot, but I'm not going to do it. I'll forget about it, but I want you to do something for me and keep your mouth shut. If you let out one word, you'll spend the rest of your days in San Quentin."

"Anything you say," said Shiny.

Redwood gave some brief instructions and handed Shiny a set of keys. Then he turned to face the window and the palm tree. A few minutes later he heard a tremendous crash and the top of the palm swayed and then disappeared from view.

"That's better," he said, staring with satisfaction at the empty space once occupied by the fronds of the palm.

"More natural." He turned around to his desk and when the phone rang, said, "Let him go. He had my permission to use the car. Just write him a ticket for careless driving and that will be it."

He felt very much better.

Eighteen

FOR MINARDI the case was solved. But Father Bredder was not satisfied because of the petunias. He had thought a great deal about the flower box with the petunias outside Bodetkin's window in the Porter Hotel and he had come to the conclusion, as he had with the books and the music, that these were flowers grown for some purpose other than the love of flowers.

There was some reasoning behind this concept. He was a flower lover himself and he knew that petunias were not a favorite of flower growers, particularly for window boxes, because they require a great deal of watering, which is messy, and are not hardy enough to resist greenfly and other pests. They were easy to raise from seed, flowered profusely, but quickly perished with any neglect. Geraniums were the best for flower boxes, and it was peculiar that Bodetkin had elected to grow petunias.

He looked the flower up in an old horticultural volume he had picked up in a secondhand bookstore and noted that it was one of the nightshade family. This information, which had at first seemed potentially important, now held no significance for him. So he thought about the petunias and the fact that they had been watered the day after Bodetkin died, and became more and more uneasy, and finally, he went round to the Porter Hotel to see Mr. Ambrose, the manager whose daughter Cynthia had re-enrolled at the Convent of the Holy Innocents, though she was having a hard time with her Latin.

Mr. Ambrose received him as before in that dark office of his which tried to maintain a quiet dignity in the face of the drabness of the rest of the hotel. He wore a tiny rose in his buttonhole as always, and it was that rose that inspired the visit.

"Delighted to see you again, Father," the manager said. "You have been through a few trials and perils since we last met, but all is solved now, I believe."

"Not everything," said Father Bredder. "I've come about the petunias."

"The petunias?" echoed Mr. Ambrose, but his air of surprise was not entirely convincing.

"Yes. Paul Bodetkin's window box of petunias." He paused. "Why did you water them after he had been killed?"

Mr. Ambrose looked at him with the kind of dismay that the priest had often seen on the face of a child at the convent trapped in a falsehood.

"How did you know?" he asked.

"Because you like flowers," said the priest. "Was that the reason you watered them? Because you knew they needed daily watering?" He put the question as he often did with children, trying out of a deep kindness to make their misdeeds at least honorable in intent.

"Yes," said Ambrose. "That and the hotel."

"The hotel?"

"I've been trying to keep it alive for decades. And it dies by centimeters every day. This hotel is my life's work. You would understand how I feel about it, I think. When Bodetkin asked me whether he could put up a window box, I first of all didn't like the idea. But then I thought it would add one touch of gaiety to the building— one little peep of color on that frontage which has grown sadder with the years. A buttonhole for an elderly person fallen on strict times." He glanced at the little rose he wore in his lapel, and the priest's heart went out to him.

"I didn't want to think of the petunias dying. They became a sort of symbol of the hotel and my struggle to keep it alive. And so I watered them. And then I became afraid and pulled them all up."

"I understand," said Father Bredder. "I hoped that was the explanation."

"Will the police . . . ?"

"No. Lieutenant Minardi will be around to ask you about how Corbini got to Bodetkin's room and how, with Bodetkin dead, he managed to get him down to his car and drive off. But he isn't interested in the petunias because he operates in a different manner." He paused. "He likes fingerprints that can be photographed," he added, but the significance of that remark was lost on Mr. Ambrose.

"I've thought about Corbini since the story appeared in the papers," said Mr. Ambrose. "It would really be very simple. The hotel staff does not come to work until eight in the morning. The room keys are out there in the open, each in its numbered pigeonhole. There are, of course, several keys for each room. It would be quite simple, before eight in the morning, for Corbini to have picked up the key to Bodetkin's room, entered, and done his business."

"But not so simple to bring him out, unobserved, after he had died of a heart attack during the struggle," said the priest.

Mr. Ambrose had recovered some of his urbanity, and he smiled slyly at Father Bredder. "The hotel laundry is collected by the staff each morning. They use a four-wheeled trolley with a large basket into which the soiled linen is put. One is placed near the elevator on every floor each night. It would not be too difficult for a man of Corbini's physique to put Bodetkin in the basket, throw a sheet over him and wheel him to the elevator, down to the ground floor and out through the rear corridor to the hotel parking lot. I think that was how it was done. The laundry trolley for that floor was missing that morning and was found in the parking lot. Nobody knew who had put it there."

"It's a pity you didn't report that," said Father Bredder.

"It's a matter of mental patterns," said Mr. Ambrose. "You as a detective would see some significance in it. I as a hotel manager would immediately suspect some lark on the part of the younger members of my small staff."

"Where is Bodetkin's window box now?" asked the priest.

"Still in place outside the window. Nothing has been touched."

"Is it very heavy?"

"Yes. I should think it would weigh at least a hundred pounds with all that earth in it. It is strongly made."

"Could I borrow one of your laundry carts?" asked the priest. "I would like to take the flower box with me. It will be returned."

"May I ask why?"

"That would spoil the surprise," said Father Bredder.

Later that evening, Minardi, departing from his usual custom, visited Father Bredder at the convent. He brought his daughter Barbara with him, perhaps as a measure of self-protection, for he was a little nervous about convents and nuns. Barbara had a present for Father Bredder, an oilskin tobacco pouch, produced by the famous firm of Dunhill.

"It's from Rick," she said. "He asked me to give it to you."

"From Rick?" exclaimed Father Bredder. "But why?"

"All he said was, 'Tell him it's for the lesson about girls.'" She examined the priest gravely. "I have to thank you, too," she said. "I wish there were millions of men like you—only not all priests."

"There are," said Father Bredder, "and I think Rick will be one of them."

For answer she flung her arms around him and, standing on tiptoe, kissed him on the cheek.

"Well," said Father Bredder. "Two presents. And the last one was the nicer. And now I have a present for you—only it's a project as well as a present. Something you'll have fun doing, and then more fun because it's to be given to someone else."

"What is it?" asked Barbara.

"That window box." He explained about it. "I thought you could replant it—I'll help—maybe with ivy geraniums. And then we could give it back to Mr. Ambrose. As a symbol that the hotel won't die."

"We could keep it planted with different things all the time," said Barbara. "But it's September. Let's use chrysanthemums first and then the ivy geranium during the winter, and in the spring we could use daffodils and hyacinths." And then, because she was a practical girl, she added, "And then you could tell Sister Lucy that I'm doing it; if I do it right, she might give me a better grade in Botany."

"She will indeed," said Father Bredder. "It will mean a lot to Mr. Ambrose. But first, we have to take out the old earth, and I fancy we will find something while we do so, which is why I asked your father to come here."

He left them a moment to go into the kitchen and returned with a hand trowel and several large brown paper sacks. He started shoveling the earth into the sacks and, when he had uncovered half the box, brought up a metal cylinder.

"This is what I thought might be there," he said.

"What's in it?" asked Barbara excitedly. "Open it quickly and see."

"No," said the priest. "That is Pandora's box. We open it to the peril of the world." He gave the cylinder to Minardi.

"I expect," he said, "That the one they found in the barge was empty?"

"No," said Minardi. "It contained film, but the cipher lacked a key."

· *183*

"Ah," said the priest. "I should have thought of that. Well, you have the key. You will turn it over to the authorities."

Minardi looked at his daughter and the priest and then at the cylinder. Something to shake the world apart. Pandora's box, indeed.

"I wish we hadn't found it," he said.

"You mustn't try to play guardian angel to the world," said Father Bredder. "That is the mistake of those who set out to help and become tyrants. God has appointed a guardian angel for the world. I don't think that's in the Scriptures anywhere, either overtly or by inference. But it's reasonable. Perhaps the guardian angel of the world is really the sum total of the guardian angels of all the people on earth. That would be quite a force."

Minardi looked at Barbara—half girl and half woman. One day she would marry a boy like Rick and bear him children, and each child, Father Bredder would say, would have a guardian angel, appointed to that station through the love of God. He felt comforted and wondered again at the extra dimension of living that Father Bredder possessed, so that angels and God and people were all mixed in one with the other.

"Let's eat," he said, because he did not like to show his emotions.

At Barbara's insistence they ate at Marty's terrible cafe, because it appeared that terrible cafes were in, as World War I was *in,* and "Red Sails in the Sunset" was *in,* and the banjo was *in,* with the mandolin pressing hard on its heels.

Marty served them himself, and the food was appalling, so Barbara was delighted with it. He shuffled over on his pain-racked feet and leaned on the table after serving each dish.

"Did you used to dance the foxtrot?" asked Barbara.

"Sure did, miss," said Marty.

"Gee, I'll bet you were good. Could you show me a little?"

"With my feet?" asked Marty. He thought a moment, shrugged elaborately and said, "What have I got to lose? I ain't danced with a pretty girl in twenty-five years." He turned to Minardi. "With your permission?" he asked, quite formally.

"Granted," said Minardi. Marty shuffled to the juke box and put on "Tea for Two" and, removing his greasy apron, led Barbara out to the tiny space between the tables and the counter.

"You got to get the rhythm," he said as he shuffled her around. "It ain't like that modern stuff. It's got a beat and a melody." His step was a little lighter and his feet didn't seem to hurt him quite so much.

Father Bredder looked at Minardi. "Some people would call that psychology," he said. "But it's far older than psychology. It's just Christianity—human kindness. The way God wants us to be. 'Tea for Two,' a pretty girl, and Marty's broken feet."